THE AMAZON STRANGER

Dave Gustaveson

YWAM Publishing

A Ministry of Youth With A Mission

P.O. Box 55787, Seattle, WA 98155
(206) 771-1153

YWAM Publishing is the publishing ministry of Youth With A Mission. Youth With A Mission (YWAM) is an international missionary organization of Christians from many denominations dedicated to presenting Jesus Christ to this generation. To this end, YWAM has focused it's efforts in three main areas: 1) Training and equipping believers for their part in fulfilling the Great Commission (Matthew 28:19). 2) Personal evangelism. 3) Mercy ministry (medical and relief work).

For a free catalog of books and materials write or call:
YWAM Publishing
P.O. Box 55787, Seattle, WA 98155
(206)771-1153 or (800) 922-2143

The Amazon Stranger

Published by Youth With A Mission Publishing
P.O. Box 55787
Seattle, WA 98155

ISBN 0-927545-83-7

Printed in the United States of America.

To my daughter Jamie
on her thirteenth birthday.
May you become everything God
designed you to be.

Other

REEL KIDS
Adventures

The Missing Video
Mystery at Smokey Mountain
The Stolen Necklace
The Mysterious Case
The Amazon Stranger
The Dangerous Voyage

Available at your local Christian bookstore or
YWAM Publishing
1(800) 922-2143

Acknowledgments

I've always admired great pioneers of the faith. Jim Elliot gave his life for the Auca Indian tribe. Against every obstacle known to man, he was radically committed to see this unreached tribe reached for Christ.

I'll never forget his famous words. "He is no fool who gives up what he cannot keep to gain what he cannot lose." Men like Don Richardson sacrificed much to reach the Sawi people as Bruchko did for the Motilone tribe.

Scores of others have followed their paths into the dangerous unknown. These whom the world is not worthy gave everything they had so the Lamb who was slain would receive the full reward for His suffering.

I trust this book will inspire others to such amazing adventures. Special thanks to Dave Irwin and his family for giving their lives for the Jarawara tribe. His insights were very helpful. Thanks to Kent and Josephine Truehl. Their visit to Los Angeles was in God's perfect timing and their understanding of Indian tribes is invaluable.

Thanks to Levi DeCarvalho and Miguel Albanez for checking over the manuscript. Special thanks to Kaye Charlotte for getting me going on this project, and Fran Poelman for the timely help. Thanks to Suzanne Howe for her encouragement, editing, and continual excitement and to Nigel Burmester for his skillful computer assistance. Thanks to Gerson Ribeiro and Dale and Suzi Olson. Thanks to Larry Wright of Procla-Media.

Thanks to the team at YWAM Publishing for maintaining clear vision for this project. Thanks to Frank Ordaz for his beautiful cover designs. And of course, to Shirley Walston for her editing skills. I always look forward to discussing the books with her and value her contributions.

And to the Lord Jesus Christ. He was part of the tribe of Judah. He longs to see every tribe, kindred, and tongue sit with Him around the throne forever.

Table of Contents

Chapter 1

The Stranger

I'm not ready to die!"

Jeff Caldwell stood speechless. He didn't know how to respond to his thirteen-year-old sister, Mindy. He ran his fingers through his rumpled blond curls, frustrated by the sudden change of plans. Traveling in the Amazon was sounding more dangerous by the moment, but he was trying to roll with the punches.

The determined fifteen-year-old took a deep breath. He glanced around the airport lounge. Under his casual blue jeans, T-shirt, and hiking boots, Jeff's tired body stiffened. He turned toward his sister. "Mindy, we talked about this. You knew this trip to the Amazon wouldn't be easy."

She pulled her shoulders back and tried to stand taller than her usual 5'4". Her hunter green blouse and jeans were mussed and wrinkled from hours of travel. Thin strands of blonde hair had escaped from the ponytail they were once tied in, hanging, defeated, on either side of her heart-shaped face. The outline of her braces showed under her clenched lips.

Jeff looked closer. Behind her stylish brown-rimmed glasses and intense brown eyes, he saw fear—the same fear that had been there when he'd helped her learn to ride her first bicycle.

At his gaze, she turned away.

He sighed and retreated. His weary blue eyes searched the crowd for Warren and K.J. Warren, their leader, was checking on flight possibilities to Labrea. As usual, Jeff's best friend K.J. was busy filming local sights.

Inside the small Brazilian airport, everything looked strange. Jeff couldn't believe they were in Porto Velho, just a few hours from a once-in-a-lifetime adventure. They were headed deep into the Amazon jungle to work with the Jarawara Indian tribe.

Mindy whirled around, interrupting Jeff's thoughts. She rubbed her puffy eyes. "Look, Jeff. I'm sorry. I feel like we've been traveling for days. Sleeping in the Manaus airport last night wiped me out. I don't want to fly on some overloaded freight flight. And don't tell me you do."

"No." Jeff shook his head. "I'd like a private jet, then a jetski for the trip up the Amazon. But those things just aren't available. We knew this trip was going to be our hardest. Remember, these people in the jungle have only been in contact with civilization for seventy years."

Mindy tried not to smile, but a tiny bit of her braces peeked through. "Okay. Okay. Don't preach to me. I've proven I can handle rough trips, haven't I?"

Jeff smiled. "I'm exhausted too. I admit that eight hours on an airport floor didn't help. But we can't stop before we even get there."

"I don't want to quit!" Mindy's face flared again. "I just think we should wait until we can get a safer flight. I don't want to fly on some broken-down cargo plane. And besides, we'll have to split up."

Jeff took a deep breath. "Look, sis. It's not my fault. There are no passenger planes available. If we don't take the cargo planes, we'll be here for days."

Stomping her foot as she turned, Mindy walked away.

Jeff glanced at his watch. It was almost one o'clock on Sunday afternoon. *Was she right?* he began to wonder. *Was this foolish?* In any case, Jeff knew Warren would make the right decision.

Warren Russell was one of Jeff's teachers at Baldwin Heights High School in the Los Angeles area. As head of the Communications Department, he had founded the Reel Kids Adventure Club a few years earlier. Warren loved taking kids to different countries, using their communication skills and sharing their faith at the same time.

The club met off campus, but had permission to use school equipment. The members, Jeff, Mindy, and Jeff's best friend K.J., were skilled in photography, video, public speaking, writing, and editing. The club produced high-quality videos to inspire others to travel to the countries they visited or to help people in need.

Communications ran in the Caldwell family. Jeff and Mindy's dad was a successful TV anchorman for a large Los Angeles station. Their mom worked as a news correspondent. Jeff's dream was to set up a high tech video production company after he graduated from college. He loved being in front of the camera.

Mindy was the ace reporter for the team. Her love for books made her an excellent researcher for their trips. Her inquisitive mind asked all the right questions. Jeff was convinced that she slept with her laptop computer.

Suddenly, Jeff saw Warren wave across the crowded airport. Warren was in his early thirties and taller than Jeff, though only by an inch. They had the same medium build. Warren's sandy brown hair was cut short enough to pass military inspection. Perhaps because he asked the club members to call him by his first name when they were away from school, people sometimes mistook him for one of the students.

Warren's soft brown eyes were always warm and friendly, communicating his attitude toward the world. On this trip, he was dressed more rugged than usual, in dark blue jeans and a blue denim shortsleeved shirt. On his feet were hiking boots that looked like they'd known hundreds of miles of trails.

Jeff glanced at Mindy as Warren joined them. He knew she was hoping for good news.

Warren's face told it all. "Sorry, you guys. For the next three days, the only planes going where we need to go are cargo planes. And they're going to be packed to the rafters with supplies."

"What does that mean?" Mindy asked warily.

"It means we'll be riding with chickens and sacks of wheat. But the good news is that neither one of them are leaving until morning. Today, we'll rest up in a hotel."

"Will we have to split up?" Mindy frowned.

"Yes. It's the only way we can do it. They're packed."

Mindy's eyes welled up with tears. "I don't want to crash."

Warren slipped an arm around her shoulder. "Why are you worried about crashing?"

"I read about jungle flights." Mindy gazed at him through her tears. "The cargo planes are the most dangerous because the pilots load them to the max. They sometimes crash."

Warren glanced at Jeff, then looked gently into her eyes. "Mindy, I would never do anything to harm you. This is our only option. Otherwise we'll have to wait for days for a plane. And traveling on land could be worse."

"We'll have to do that anyway when we get to Labrea," Jeff added.

"By boat you mean." Mindy laughed nervously. "And what about the alligators along the river?"

Warren grinned and threw up his hands. "We'll just have to stay in the canoe, won't we? You have to admit it will make dramatic video footage—especially the alligators." He laughed. "I had hoped we could fly directly to the village airstrip, but all the missionary planes are either scheduled elsewhere or in for repairs. But I've been assured a plane will take us out at the end of our trip."

"Well, at least we'll get some rest today," Mindy said, shaking her finger. "But I'm still not comfortable with this."

"We have prayed a lot about this trip," Jeff pointed out. "God called us here. He'll protect us...just like He always does."

"We'd better get our stuff together," Warren said. "We're all really tired. Anybody know where K.J is?"

"A minute ago he was over there with a camera attached to his face," Mindy said, pointing.

Jeff had to smile when he saw K.J. racing toward them. His hands held the Canon Hi-8 camcorder securely, but with every step, straps flew and bags bobbed against his body.

Jeff noticed girls in the airport watching K.J. and giggling. His slick, black hair, constant smile, and dark, mischievous eyes made him look like he was up to something. At home, girls sometimes thought 5'6" was too short, but here in Brazil, he fit right in.

Kyle James Baxter had been Jeff's best friend since fifth grade, when the Caldwells had moved to Baldwin Heights. K.J. was never afraid to try something new. Over the years, he'd often gotten them both in trouble. When Warren had first proposed the Reel Kids Club, Jeff knew K.J. would make the perfect cameraman. For a fourteen-year-old, he had an excellent eye for style and design.

Now, K.J. skidded to a halt in front of them. "I've been talking to a British man, kind of a strange guy. He's heading to the same area we are and says we're in for a wild adventure."

"What do you mean?" Mindy cried.

"He told me the river trip from Labrea is pretty tough."

"Oh great," Mindy snapped. "If we survive the plane ride, we'll die on the river."

Warren put his hands up to calm everybody. "We don't have any choice. We can't fly in. People go up the river all the time."

"What'd you find out, K.J.?" Jeff asked.

"Not much. The man said his family used to live near the Jara...you know...the tribe we're visiting. How do you say that name again?"

"Ya-da-wa-da," Mindy said one syllable at a time while rolling her eyes. "Jarawara isn't spelled much like it's pronounced."

"Okay, okay. I remember now. Anyway, this guy still owns property there. He's going back on business."

"What was strange about him?" Jeff wanted to know.

"He asked weird questions. I couldn't figure out where he was coming from."

"How old was he?" Mindy asked.

"Probably in his late fifties," K.J. said. "He has his own plane. He's flying right to the village."

"Lucky guy." Mindy groaned. "Does he have any empty seats?"

Everyone laughed. Warren looked at his watch. "It's nearly two. We need to find a hotel. We can use all the rest we can get for the long day tomorrow."

Suddenly, K.J. pulled on Warren's arm and pointed. "Look, there's the guy I talked to. Let me introduce you. Maybe he'll tell us more."

Jeff watched his friend run over to a tall man in a tan safari suit. His shiny briefcase and neatly polished shoes looked slightly out of place.

As he approached with K.J., the man held his head high. Little round glasses were perched on his nose. His sideburns and thick moustache were grey. His large, dark eyes had a mystery about them, as if he were deep in thought.

K.J. introduced the team members.

"Nice to meet you," the man said. "My name is Mr. Giles. Your friend told me you're visiting one of the tribes."

"Yes," Warren said with a smile. "We're a video club filming with Dr. Jones. He runs a medical clinic and has worked with the Jarawara tribe for fifteen years."

Mr. Giles's eyes darkened, and he was silent.

"Do you know Dr. Jones?" Warren asked slowly, noticing the sudden change.

"Yes," Mr. Giles replied. "I'm afraid so."

Confused, Jeff looked Mr. Giles straight in the eye. "What do you mean?"

Mr. Giles looked at his watch. "I'm sorry," he stuttered. "I don't have time to talk. I must catch my plane. Maybe I'll see you in the jungle."

"Nice to meet you," Warren said with a smile.

Everyone else slowly nodded.

Mr. Giles started to walk away, but he turned back. His eyes narrowed, and his face tightened. "I have one more thing to say."

Everyone waited quietly.

"I wouldn't travel on that river if I were you."

"Why's that?" Mindy asked.

Mr. Giles looked angry. "You don't know what you're doing. If you're smart, you'll turn around and go home."

"What do you mean?" Mindy demanded.

Mr. Giles ignored her. "Your friend says you're taking a cargo plane into Labrea. Too dangerous."

"Why's that?" Jeff asked.

"The runway is short. The plane has to dive at the last minute. Cargo planes don't do that very well."

Everyone stared nervously at each other. Mr. Giles seemed pleased with himself. "If you survive that, you'll get lost in the jungle. But that's not the worst part."

"What's that?" Mindy whispered.

"The canoe ride. Most of them tip over. If you do, you'll be lunch for a hungry 'gator."

Chapter 2

Heavy Flight

Everyone watched the stranger hurry away.

"K.J.," Mindy snapped, "I'm not sure about the friends you pick."

"It must've been something you said," K.J. retorted. "He was friendly before."

"He didn't like it when we mentioned Dr. Jones," Warren pointed out. "And he was definitely trying to frighten us."

"It worked." Mindy's eyes looked like they were about to pop through her glasses.

"We've come too far to be frightened by that guy," Jeff said.

Warren looked at his watch. "Let's go find a hotel. We'll think more clearly after a good night's sleep."

Mindy picked up her backpack and draped it over her shoulder. "Maybe you're right. I think I could sleep forever."

The team dragged themselves through the airport lounge to find a taxi.

❖ ❖ ❖ ❖ ❖ ❖ ❖

Early Monday morning, the team made their way back to the airport. They quickly found the area of the runway where the small planes were being loaded. Moving closer, Jeff couldn't believe his eyes. Among the boxes and cartons outside the small Brazilian Piper planes sat three bloody sides of beef, an icy tray of frozen fish, and small piles of vegetables.

Then he noticed Mindy. She looked as frozen as the fish, and her mouth was open almost as wide as her eyes. "Don't tell me these are the other passengers!" she yelled. "Where are we supposed to sit?"

"These are cargo planes, Mindy." Warren chuckled. "It's one of the ways they get supplies to Labrea."

"Well," K.J. said, focusing his camera, "I'm sure they'll store this stuff in the back of the plane. Sure makes a great shot, though."

As Jeff, Mindy, K.J., and Warren waited, pilots and cargo loaders looked the team over. Some even snickered.

Jeff chose to ignore them. Instead, he asked a

question that had been bugging him all morning. "Warren, why do you think Mr. Giles got upset when we mentioned Dr. Jones?"

"I don't know. Dr. Jones is a good man. He's a doctor who's worked with the tribe for over fifteen years."

K.J. put down the camera for a second. "Maybe the guy was just tired. You're making a big deal over nothing."

Jeff watched the Brazilian workers lift the meat inside the plane. "Still, we need to be on our spiritual toes," he said slowly. "Something is up. Mr. Giles definitely had a problem with Dr. Jones. Maybe we'll find out something when we get there."

"According to my research," Mindy added, "Mr. Giles is right about the treacherous landing in Labrea. I don't think I can handle getting lost in the jungle. And I don't even want to think about the alligators!"

"He did his best to frighten us." Jeff nodded his head. "But God is bigger than any of those things. Besides, Dr. Jones said we should go up the river if we couldn't catch a plane. He wouldn't have said that if it was really dangerous. He would have told us to wait for a plane."

"You're right about that, Jeff," Warren said. "Let's get our stuff in the plane. There's only room for two passengers in each plane, so Jeff will fly with Mindy and I'll go with K.J."

"Cool." K.J. smiled. "Maybe I can film you guys from the air."

"I'm glad I'm going with my brother," Mindy said to K.J. "I'd be scared to death in that plane with you and your camera."

❖❖❖❖❖❖❖

Near the planes, Jeff and the others found a shady spot to pray. Jeff suddenly realized how hot it was. Sweat dripped from his forehead even though it was early in the morning.

"Jeff, why don't you lead us?" Warren suggested.

Jeff bowed his head. "Lord, we can't figure out what's going on, but we know You have everything under control. Please be with us on this trip."

Everyone uttered an amen.

"And Lord," Jeff went on, "we know You love every tribe. Please give us an opportunity to share Your love. Let us be a blessing to Dr. Jones in his work."

Mindy squeezed Jeff's hand, wanting to pray. "Lord," she began, "if there is any truth to that alligator story, please throw them a banquet before we get there."

Grinning at each other, they wiped off their sweaty hands.

"How long do you think it will take once we get to Labrea?" K.J. asked.

Warren pulled out the directions Dr. Jones had given him. "We should get to Labrea around nine. Then it will take a couple of hours to go up the Perus River by canoe and outboard motor."

"And where are we going to get an outboard?" Mindy wanted to know.

"I wondered about that, too," Warren replied. "But Dr. Jones says we can rent a boat and driver when we arrive. We'll see."

"How far can we go on that?" K.J. asked.

"To a village called Samaumo. There's a Brazilian guide there who sometimes works with Dr. Jones. He'll be watching for us to take us to the village."

"How far is the Jarawara village from Samaumo?" Jeff asked.

"About three hours. We'll hike most of the way, but first we take a motorized canoe up an inlet until it runs out."

"What does that mean?" Mindy's eyes grew wide.

"When we come to the end of the water, we walk the rest of the way—about two hours. We should get there before dark."

"That doesn't sound so bad." Mindy twisted her face, calculating the length of the journey. "Maybe Mr. Giles was just trying to scare us."

Two Brazilian pilots suddenly began calling in Portuguese. Jeff saw them waving for the team to get on board. Mindy hugged Warren and K.J. and followed Jeff to the plane.

When his eyes adjusted to the semi-darkness inside the plane, Jeff couldn't believe what he saw. Mindy just gasped. The inside of the plane was cold and packed full of vegetables. The air reeked with the smells of raw meat and fish. Jeff looked for seats but found only a board propped on top of some boxes. An unwrapped side of beef lay beside them, dripping blood all over the floor of the plane.

"I'm not going," Mindy cried, turning toward the door. "I'm outta here."

But just as she tried to move, the door shut.

"Too late, sis." Jeff gave her a reassuring smile. "Boy, I'm seeing the price missionaries pay to win a tribe for Jesus. These Jarawara people must be special."

"I don't think I'm called to work with a tribe." Mindy held her nose.

Jeff squeezed his nose too. "Sis, I've heard missionaries say that once God puts His love for a people in your heart, He gives you the grace to reach them."

"I'm gonna need lots of grace for this trip," she pouted.

Looking out the small window, Jeff saw Warren and K.J. climb into the other Piper. He knew K.J. would love filming the makeshift seats and cargo in his plane.

Suddenly, the roar of the propellers drowned out any further conversation. All Jeff could do was give his frightened sister a "thumbs up." Inside, he was frightened too—perhaps more frightened than he had ever been.

They held onto old, worn straps that hung from the ceiling of the plane. As the plane taxied down the runway, Jeff prayed. He wondered if the Piper was too heavily loaded to get off the ground.

The trees raced by as the plane went faster and faster. Jeff had experienced small plane rides before, but it had never taken this long to get off the ground. Mindy's grip kept tightening on his arm.

He held his breath, offering another quick prayer. Finally the wheels lifted off the ground, and Jeff and Mindy both let out sighs of relief. The plane climbed higher and higher. Looking out the window, Jeff watched Porto Velho begin to disappear.

Jeff knew they were in the state of Amazonis. As far as he could see into the distance, there was nothing but the tops of trees and many rivers winding like dull ribbons through them. Beside him, Mindy was studying everything too.

After nearly an hour of nothing but treetops and rivers, things below became more clear. Jeff pointed to the trees when he noticed different shades of green. Some of them bloomed with pink, red, and bright yellow flowers, adding beauty and majesty to the rain forest.

Jeff and Mindy had both studied about the rain forest. They knew much of it was being cut down and destroyed by greedy developers.

Rivers intersected below them. Some looked brown, others black. As the plane began to descend, Jeff and Mindy spotted a stream and a tiny airstrip.

Jeff pointed to the people along the river. They were waving as the planes flew over. Automatically, Jeff and Mindy waved back.

As they got closer, the river appeared bigger and bigger. Mindy smiled. "Hey, I recognize this," she said. "This must be the Perus River. It's one of the longest, windiest rivers in the world—especially in the Amazon region. Samaumo is on this river, and it floods the area out in the rainy season."

Jeff nodded, then felt a sudden plunge. His stomach swirled. He quickly looked at Mindy, who had turned white. It felt like the plane was diving straight down. Looking out the small window, he couldn't believe it. Palm trees were beside them now. He closed his eyes, afraid one of the wings was going to clip a branch at any moment.

Suddenly, Mindy and Jeff both slid off the board. They crashed and bumped into some sacks of grain at their feet. Jeff glanced at Mindy, who had grabbed his hand on the way down. Her eyes were closed, and her face was tightened into a knot.

Jeff's mind raced faster and faster. He couldn't shake Mr. Giles's words from his mind. Expecting a crash, he forced his eyes open.

The plane's wheels hit something, then they bounced back into the air. A split second later, they hit again. To Jeff's surprise, it felt like a runway. He and Mindy both let out huge sighs of relief. They were safely on the ground in Labrea.

As the pilot slammed on the brakes, Jeff said a quick thanks to God, then prayed the other plane would make it.

The plane taxied down the short runway, and Jeff stretched up to look out of the front window. He could see thick jungle ahead as well as a tiny airport building. He relaxed, knowing they would be there soon.

Suddenly, Jeff noticed two men in military uniforms followed by two men in suits coming from the small building. They looked serious.

And they were heading straight for Jeff and Mindy's plane.

Chapter 3

Red Tape

For a brief second, Jeff wished he was in the air again. He groaned, dreading the open door. What did these men want? They couldn't be after the team. It had to be a mistake. How could anybody know they were there?

Jeff's mind raced with questions while the pilot moved toward the door. Mindy had spotted the military men and looked confused. As the pilot pulled on the door, he mumbled something in Portuguese. He looked back at Mindy and Jeff with a smirk on his face, as if he were angry.

There must be a problem with the pilot or the

plane, Jeff thought. The pilot must be in some kind of trouble. Just then, the other plane pulled up next to them. Jeff was glad to see Warren.

The soldiers moved closer to the door, then the pilot opened it. Mindy finally let go of the straps and prepared to get out. Jeff sat still and hoped for the best.

An angry-looking man yelled at both pilots for a minute, then he stuck his head inside. "Get out, please," he commanded. He was an older gentleman in a blue suit.

Jeff glanced at Mindy, who was shaking her head. They climbed off the plane slowly, trying not to kick out the bunches of carrots that had scattered on the floor.

Once outside, the men ordered Jeff, Mindy, K.J., and Warren to wait while the pilots unloaded the luggage. Then they were all led inside.

No one on the team understood Portuguese, so they had no idea what was happening. Dr. Jones knew the language well and would be their interpreter once they got to the tribe, but until then, they were at the mercy of these men.

Inside the tiny office, the four of them sat on some old wooden benches. Jeff glanced at Warren. He had never seen their leader panic. He realized that Warren's unwavering faith was one of the things he most admired about him. Mindy just looked confused, and K.J. sat still for a change, with his camera bag cradled in his lap.

The older official walked up and addressed them in English. "We understand you are here to film an Indian tribe."

Jeff was shocked. How does he know? he wondered.

"Yes, that's right," Warren replied, snapping open his briefcase and reaching inside. He grabbed a file folder. "We're a communications team from Los Angeles. We're called the Reel Kids Club, and we're on our way to visit the Jarawara tribe."

The official became angry. "You didn't think you could film them, did you?"

Warren looked surprised. "Yes, sir, we did."

"Who gave you permission?" he asked.

Warren shuffled through his papers. "Sir, I'm looking for documents giving us permission to film the tribe. We're making a documentary that will educate Americans on tribes in the Amazon."

"We have no record of this," the official replied sternly. The other man in the suit quietly watched the scene, while the soldiers stood guard outside.

A smile suddenly appeared on Warren's face. "Here it is," he said, pulling a paper out of the file. "The National Indian Foundation gave us permission."

In an outburst of rage, the official grabbed the paper. "Let me see this!"

Everyone waited patiently as the man read. K.J. clutched his camera bag tightly.

"I'm sorry," said the official, looking up from the paper. "We don't have a copy of this in our records. You could have written it yourself. Normally we don't do this but I have no choice. I am going to confiscate your equipment until this can be verified."

Warren's face grew red. Jeff knew their leader had lots of self-control, but he could see it wearing thin.

"Sir," Warren spoke calmly but firmly, "I demand to see your supervisor. We spent months filing the proper paperwork to get permission. The Indian Foundation was happy when they heard what we wanted to do."

"I'm sorry." The official frowned. "Our office is closed on Monday. If you desire, you may come back to appeal later in the week. But for now, I must take your equipment. If we catch you filming in Amazonis without permission, we will throw you in jail."

K.J.'s face fell. Jeff knew his best friend would rather give up girls than his camera equipment.

Mindy's eyes narrowed. "I wonder if Mr. Giles had anything to do with this. K.J., why did you tell him what we were doing?"

"Wait a minute." Warren held up his hand. "I don't see how he could have done this. But even if he did, it's not K.J.'s fault. We have nothing to hide."

Jeff noticed that the official was listening closely to their conversation. He wondered if Mr. Giles really was responsible for this.

"Hand over your video equipment," the official suddenly commanded. "All of it. Unless you want us to search your belongings."

Warren nodded toward K.J.'s camera bag. "We'll have to cooperate. I'll come back with Dr. Jones as soon as we can to straighten this mess out."

K.J. slowly unzipped the bag on his lap. Lovingly, he pulled out his camcorder, videotapes, and spare batteries. Like a toddler giving up his favorite toy, he laid each piece on the table.

"There," K.J. said when he was through. "Please promise you'll take good care of them."

"You have our word," the official said. "You'll get everything back when you prove you have permission."

The team filed slowly out of the office. K.J. looked depressed, and Mindy was frightened again.

"Something's going on here," Jeff said. "I don't get it. All we're doing is visiting an Indian tribe."

"Look." Warren stopped everyone. "This might just be a big mistake. Let's not try to figure out some sinister plot that might not be there."

Mindy looked at her brother. "I don't see how they knew we were coming. Or why they care."

Warren stopped again. "The National Indian Foundation may have second thoughts about our filming project. Dr. Jones knows them. He'll know who to talk to and how to straighten this out."

K.J. groaned. "What about the footage I could have gotten on our trip in? I'll never get another opportunity for canoes, crocodiles, and swamps!"

"I forgot about that," Warren said. "Maybe you can go with us when we come back here."

"That's a good idea." K.J.'s eyes lit up. "Anyway, they didn't take my still camera. I can get some decent shots with it."

"Great, K.J." Warren smiled. "That's the spirit."

Outside the airport office, taxicabs, horses, and wagons stood waiting for passengers. Jeff turned to the others. "I'm getting hungry."

Warren laughed. "So am I. Let's get a snack on the way to the boat. It should take about two hours to get to Samauma from here. Then Dr. Jones's friend, Miguel, will guide us the rest of the way to the Jarawara village."

❖❖❖❖❖❖❖

Jeff stared at the twelve-foot aluminum boat. Scrapes, dents, and missing chips of paint showed years of abuse. The rusty twenty-five horsepower motor looked like an antique. He hoped it would get them up the river.

The Brazilian driver didn't speak much English, but Warren communicated with hand gestures and notes. After paying fifteen U.S. dollars, the team got their things ready for the ride to Samaumo.

Standing on the dock, they waited for the driver to finish loading the last of their stuff. K.J. was busy with his camera, photographing every detail.

Watching him, Jeff laughed. "K.J. doesn't miss a trick."

"Nope," Warren replied. "That's why he's our cameraman."

"If he just didn't get us into...," Mindy muttered.

Jeff quickly put his finger to his mouth to quiet Mindy. "He's doing great, sis. So far, so good."

"I'm nervous about our trip up the river," Mindy admitted. "Maybe Mr. Giles was right. He was right about that plane ride."

"This part of the trip will be fine," Warren pointed out. "It's a hired boat."

"What about the canoe trip?" Mindy asked.

"It's hired too," Warren said. "But the river inlet is a little trickier to move on."

The boat driver waved for them to come on board. Gingerly, they stepped into the boat and started up the river. Jeff kept staring at the banks on either side of him. He couldn't believe how wide the river was.

"What do you know about the Perus River, sis?"

Mindy knew exactly where to look. Reaching in a bag, she pulled out her research notebook. "It's one of the twenty biggest rivers in the world. It's longer than the Mississippi—and that runs all the way from Minnesota to New Orleans. It's also one of the world's windiest rivers."

Looking ahead, Jeff saw the river going for a ways then curling back and forth. The overworked outboard motor screamed along, and the boat bounced over the muddy water.

"Why is it called the Perus River?" Jeff asked.

"The Perus Indians used to live in a large area. They are gone now, but a few tribes are descendants of theirs."

"What about the Jarawara Indians?" Jeff wanted to know. "Are they related to the Perus?"

"I don't think so," Mindy said. "There are thousands of tribes in these jungles. Some have never seen a Brazilian, let alone a white man."

Around them, houses stood high off the ground on stilts. It reminded Jeff of his old tree house. Along the banks, people were busy fixing homes and houseboats. Children played, and women worked. Piles of logs were everywhere. K.J. snapped shots of it all.

"This dense jungle makes the perfect background for my shots," he said, reloading his camera. "I'll bet this place floods during the rainy season."

Mindy smiled. "According to my notes, the waters rise as high as fifty meters from December to May, during their rainy season. That's why those houses are back a ways from the river and are built on stilts."

"Wow," K.J. said as he took pictures of them.

Mindy looked over her notes. "I'm dreading hiking into the jungle to get to the Jarawaras' village—some place called the flood basin."

As she filled them in about what to expect, Jeff shook his head in admiration. He was always impressed with his sister's research. Upstream, he caught a glimpse of a large community.

Jeff motioned to the boat driver and pointed. "Is this Samaumo?"

The boat driver laughed and nodded his head.

"I'm really hungry," Mindy said.

Warren looked at his watch. "It's almost one. Dr. Jones said Miguel would look for us at the dock. Let's find something for lunch. If we get to the canoe by two, we should make it to the village by dark."

❖ ❖ ❖ ❖ ❖ ❖ ❖

The team finished a big lunch of beans, rice, and beef and headed to the dock. Upon arriving, Jeff saw several primitive canoes that had been carved or cut out of single trees. Looking them over carefully, he tried to imagine how big the trees must have been.

Mindy gulped, but didn't say a word. K.J. knelt on the dock to change his film.

Suddenly, Jeff felt someone staring at him. Turning, he noticed a short, stocky Brazilian man looking right at him. The man's hair and eyes were a shade darker than the stains on his khaki shirt.

Ever so slightly, the man tipped his brown hat in Jeff's direction, but his eyes remained icy cold. Jeff shifted uncomfortably from foot to foot. He watched out of the corner of his eye, but the man never took his eyes off their group.

Maybe this guy is our guide, Jeff thought. Boldly, he moved over to talk to the man. "Excuse me, sir. Do you speak English?"

The man stared coldly into Jeff's eyes but didn't move a muscle. Jeff tried again. "Do you understand English? Are you the guide Dr. Jones sent?"

The man laughed in Jeff's face. "Do I look like your guide?" the man growled. "I'm waiting for the next canoe—just like you."

Jeff couldn't believe his almost-perfect English. He wondered how the man knew they wanted a canoe.

The man looked away, disgusted. Jeff noticed a paper in his clenched fist. He couldn't believe his eyes.

Written across the top was the name "Mr. Giles."

Chapter 4

The Canoe Ride

Jeff didn't know what to do. He stood frozen as the strange, dark-featured Brazilian turned away.

Jeff noticed that Mindy had been watching them. He walked over to her quickly and grabbed her arm. "Did you see the name on that paper?" he whispered.

"No," Mindy said. "Why?"

"It said *Mr. Giles.* "

Mindy's eyes grew wide. "Well, maybe he works for him or something."

"You're right. He'll probably be on the same canoe as us. The name over his shirt pocket was Manuel Santanos. That must be his name."

Warren joined the group. He had been finalizing the arrangements for their canoe trip. Jeff explained what had happened.

Warren looked a little troubled. "There isn't anything we can do at this point. We'll just keep an eye on him."

"Maybe he's keeping an eye on us." Jeff was still shaking a little. "I'm not so sure I want to get on the same canoe as him."

Warren had everyone sit down. "It'll be okay. We've traveled for two days, and nothing will stop us now. We're only a few hours from Dr. Jones, and I know he's anxious to get the medical supplies in those boxes. We just need to wait for our guide to show up."

"Let's pray again," Jeff suggested.

Everyone bowed their head as Warren offered a quick prayer. Jeff smiled at Mindy as they all said an amen. "Well. We wanted adventure. This is it."

Mindy tried to grin. K.J. laughed.

The heavy wooden canoes were nearly ready to depart. Jeff recognized the Briggs and Stratton engines from his lawn-mowing days, but he hadn't ever seen one with a ten-foot shaft and propeller at the end. Each canoe only held four or five passengers, so the team would have to split up like they had on the cargo planes.

Jeff turned to K.J. "Mindy said there are twenty-eight varieties of piranha in the Amazon. They have teeth like little saws and can strip off a person's flesh in minutes."

Mindy gave Jeff a dirty look, then became real quiet.

Jeff grinned. "It's okay, Mindy. I understand the Brazilian people fish for piranha."

K.J. laughed, making sure Mindy was listening. "Don't mess with them. They travel in large schools, you know. If you fall in, you'd better hope school isn't in session."

Jeff joined in K.J.'s laughter. "Yeah. But I hear they're not really as vicious as they are in the movies."

"Let's hope we don't find out," K.J. said.

Suddenly, a tall, dark Brazilian man with a backpack walked up. He smiled at Jeff and extended his hand. "You must be the club from California."

Everyone nodded and shook hands.

"My name is Miguel Santana," the man said. "I'm a friend of Dr. Jones. He and I sometimes work together on behalf of the Jarawara. He said you'd be here today if you couldn't get a plane. I'm glad to guide you. And to have company on the way to the village."

"Looks like you're just in time," Warren said. "The canoes will be departing soon."

Jeff felt better now and knew Mindy did too. K.J. smiled from ear to ear. But the stranger in the brown hat was still staring their way.

The kids spent the next few minutes explaining to Miguel about the club, their trip, and the strange man. Then the canoers finished packing their freight and waved that it was time to go.

Miguel pointed to the back canoe. "Warren, if you and K.J. want to ride in that one with the freight, I'll stay with Mindy and Jeff in this one."

Jeff squirmed when the strange Brazilian man

climbed in behind Miguel. "Why do they use such long shafts?" Jeff asked, trying to ignore the man.

Miguel smiled. "This is a pretty tough trip. It's different than the Perus River. There are lots of trees and garbage in this waterway. The shaft has to be long enough to lift the propeller out of the water to clean it if it gets clogged."

Jeff decided to relax and enjoy the trip, even though he still could feel the man watching him.

K.J. waved from the other canoe. "I'm glad this is gonna be a short trip."

"We'll be okay," Warren said. "Just don't rock the boat."

As the canoe pushed away from the dock, Jeff held his breath. Mindy's body stiffened, and she sat perfectly still. The other canoe followed.

Looking over the side, Jeff saw only two inches of the canoe sticking out of the water. He sat motionless as they gained speed.

The pilot nosed skillfully around floating branches, rocks, and even sandbars. Then he handed everyone an empty coconut shell.

"What's this for?" Jeff asked.

"Bailing water." Miguel laughed. "Sometimes the boat leaks or gets swamped."

Jeff hoped Mindy hadn't heard that. *Maybe Mr. Giles was right,* Jeff thought. He glanced back at the strange man, who was lounging against the side of the canoe, his hands behind his head. The pilot wore a big smile and a Panama hat as they putt-putted up the inlet.

Moments later, the canoe struggled through some high grass. The engine screamed louder and louder. The canoe suddenly felt unbalanced to Jeff, like a car twisted in an accident. All at once, water began rushing in around their feet. The canoe was tipping. Jeff's stomach flip-flopped. *We're sinking!* he thought. The driver yelled in Portuguese.

Miguel started bailing as fast as he could. It didn't take Jeff and Mindy long to figure out what to do.

Jeff grabbed the coconut shell, scooped up water from the bottom of the canoe, and dumped it back into the river. Praying hard, he saw the water rushing over the sides. Between scoopfuls, Jeff caught a glimpse of the stranger's evil grin.

Mindy couldn't hold back her tears. She bailed and cried at the same time. Jeff knew the slightest move could capsize the whole canoe. He relaxed a bit when the driver steered the canoe closer to the shore, where they would be able to bail the water out.

Suddenly, Jeff gasped. Right in the path of the canoe were four large, menacing alligators perched on top of a fallen tree. Mindy screamed. Jeff prayed frantically, noticing Miguel looked frightened too.

The canoe moved straight toward the alligators. Jeff wondered what the driver would do. Water was still rushing in, and the rear canoe couldn't help them now.

The alligators' eight-foot, hard-shelled bodies looked like terrifying fortress of strength. Jeff stared into four rows of white teeth lining four red mouths.

Suddenly, a noise filled the jungle: "Ummm-mmmm bah! Ummmmmmmm bah-yah-yah!"

It came from the alligators. The canoe was heading right into the middle of an alligator colony.

"We're in for it now!" Mindy squealed. "Mr. Giles was telling the truth!"

Instantly, Jeff turned to the man behind them. He looked frightened too, but Jeff still thought he saw a slight snicker on his face.

The driver screamed in Portuguese and tried to steer around the alligators. Mindy covered her eyes. Everyone but the stranger bailed frantically. The canoe was still full of water, but at least they were moving away from the alligators.

Suddenly, two large alligators slid silently into the river. They headed straight for the canoe. Jeff knew they were in trouble now. In his head he could hear Mr. Giles's warning screaming over and over.

Jeff looked toward heaven, making a desperate cry. Both alligators' eyeballs and snouts appeared on the surface of the water, but they swam past the canoe.

Mindy gasped in relief. Jeff was shocked. He turned to see Warren relax and K.J. lower the camera from his face. K.J.'s eyes and his grin were huge with excitement, but his face was as white as a sheet. Jeff just shook his head. Amazingly, K.J. had taken pictures of the whole thing.

The canoe came to a stop. Gradually the "ummmmmmmm bah!" chorus died away. They continued bailing until the canoe was ready to go again.

As they began moving on the river again, Jeff didn't even want to think of the other dangerous animals in the water—piranha, snakes, and who knew what else.

Jeff looked at Miguel, who was smiling again.

The danger had passed, at least for now. Jeff looked at his watch. It was two in the afternoon. Overhead, the sun was still shining, but the forest became darker and darker as the trees became thicker along the banks.

Large trees and dense foliage closed in on both sides. Jeff looked ahead. It didn't seem possible for the canoe to get through the small inlet. He watched insects of every kind flying around them. It made him glad they had applied insect repellant earlier.

Yet even in the darkness, there was beauty. He saw a web of gigantic spiders. Then he heard a swarm of busy bees. *This is another world,* he thought. Mindy finally smiled when she saw two small brown monkeys jumping in the trees.

Suddenly, the canoe stopped. The driver yelled something in Portuguese.

Jeff turned to Miguel. "What's he saying now?"

"He's got to back up. There is too much junk in the way. He's got to get through over there."

The driver had taken an inlet that was too narrow. Jeff glanced back at the staring stranger, who was laughing again. Mindy had her head down. Jeff wondered how much more she could take. The driver yelled for the other canoe to back up.

The engines howled and moaned as the canoes strained backward. Jeff checked the bottom of their boat to see if water was coming in again.

The canoe inched back. The engine sputtered. Jeff turned to Miguel who pointed to the propeller. "It's picked up too much grass. He's got to clean the propeller."

Jeff couldn't believe this was happening. He

wondered if missionaries always went through stuff like this to get to the tribes. He had a whole new admiration for those who left their homes to tell other people about Jesus.

The driver picked up the shaft. After cleaning off slimy grass and mud the color of nutmeg, he tried again.

Jeff looked around, watching for more alligators. Mindy held the coconut husk in her hand, ready to bail at the slightest splash of water.

"It's been a tough trip," Miguel said to Jeff, "but Dr. Jones is looking forward to your coming. He's a good man."

"Does he get many visitors?" Jeff asked.

"Not many." Miguel smiled. "Usually only people carrying supplies and mail. Life can get lonely out here."

"Do you work with him all the time?"

"No. Only on special assignments like this. I've got great respect for him. He's done lot of good for the Jarawara people."

The canoes finally started moving again. After a few minutes, the strange man spoke to the driver. He nodded and pointed the canoe toward the river bank.

"What did he say?" Jeff asked Miguel.

"He wants out here. He must know a shortcut to wherever he's going. We'll stay on for a few more minutes."

Jeff nodded, not taking his eyes off the man.

As the man hopped out of the canoe, he turned to Jeff and Mindy and laughed. Jeff sat frozen. Mindy looked the other way.

The man stood on the shore, looking right at Jeff. He tipped his hat and then turned into the forest.

"Your troubles have just begun," he called over his shoulder.

Chapter 5

Jungle Muck

Jeff watched the stranger disappear into the dense jungle. "What did he mean by that?"

A serious look came over Miguel's face. "Something is going on here. I think he was sent to frighten you guys."

"He did," Mindy said. "But why would anyone want to scare us?"

No one had an answer. They sat silent...wondering.

As they continued on their trip, the inlet narrowed—as if the forest had swallowed the river. Only one canoe could pass between the banks. Soon they bumped up against land.

"This is as far as we go," Miguel said, picking up his backpack and stepping out of the canoe.

The canoe drivers neatly piled Dr. Jones's supplies, then pushed off to return to Samaumo.

"Whew. I'm glad that's over." Jeff stretched.

Everyone nodded in agreement.

Miguel pointed ahead. "We'll go along the inlet a ways to the trail. Dr. Jones will send some men to pick up the supplies."

Everyone followed Miguel into a relatively open space, near a small grove of squat palm trees. Their rough trunks were a yard or more in diameter. Jeff looked up. Like huge brown corncobs, they rose about fifteen feet in the air. At the top, the branches spread out, laden with broad green leaves.

The water of the inlet had been cooling while it lasted, but in the clearing, the midday sun was unbearable. Jeff wiped sweat from his forehead. He ducked under dense foliage whenever he could.

Beyond the fat, spaced palms, the vast jungle trees stood like a living wall, rising to a height of sixty feet or more. As if they were holding hands, a network of branches and vines clasped together high above the palm leaves.

The air was heavy and strong with the moldy odors of dying things. On the damp earth Jeff could see fallen palm branches and half-decayed leaves. Scattered ferns drooped in the humidity. Broken, empty shells of palm nuts, their meat eaten away by hungry animals, had been strewn over the clearing to rot and nourish the soil.

Overhead, Jeff often couldn't find a patch of sky. He saw only a dome of trees and the vines that hung from them into their path.

Suddenly, Miguel stopped them. "Before we get too far into the forest, I should tell you to stick together on the trail. Wild animals won't bother us if we stay close."

"Wild animals?" Mindy asked in a squeaky voice.

"Yes," Miguel answered. "We might see a snake or two, wild pigs, maybe even a jaguar or panther. People rarely get hurt if they're in a group."

Mindy ran closer to Jeff, who was behind Miguel. "You can count on me staying close."

"Me too," K.J. echoed, as he caught up.

As they moved deeper into the jungle, Jeff heard a very familiar noise. "Mosquitos!" he cried. "Can we stop a minute? I need more repellant."

They all stopped, and Jeff pulled out a can of spray as swarms of mosquitos snarled an angry chorus. The team covered any exposed skin.

Miguel laughed. "You guys will be able to write a book about this trip."

"That's for sure," Mindy said as she tried to swat some of the buzzing critters. "A big book."

"The mosquitos are bad in certain places," Miguel added. "There aren't many at the village."

Jeff, Mindy, K.J., even Warren sighed in relief.

"We're coming to a marshy section soon," Miguel warned. "It will take about twenty minutes to cross."

"What do you mean?" Mindy cried. "Another obstacle course?"

"This will be the last one," Miguel assured her. "Then it's a half hour hike to the village."

Jeff looked at his watch. It was nearly four. The

sunlight was breaking through overhead, and he was hot.

Ahead, Jeff saw what looked like a logging site. The ground was thick with young trees, about four to six inches in diameter. Their branches had been removed, and they were laid side by side.

"That looks weird," Jeff said. "What is it?"

"That's the marshy area I told you about," Miguel said. "This whole area floods during the rainy season. It gets completely covered with water—all the way up to where the Jarawaras live."

As Jeff got closer, what he thought was earth was really thick black muck. "How deep is that stuff?"

Miguel laughed. "Don't try to figure it out. I've pushed poles down there and haven't hit bottom.

"We walk across it?" Mindy asked. "You mean the logs are like a bridge?"

"Well, yes. The logs are a bridge," Miguel said with a grin. "Except they aren't connected in any way. And yes, we have to cross it if we want to get to the village. You'll be okay." He tapped Mindy under the chin to close her mouth.

Miguel grabbed some long, sturdy sticks laying along the marsh and handed two sticks to everyone. "Use these like ski poles. They'll help with your balance."

"What happens if we fall in?" Mindy cried.

"See you later." K.J. laughed.

"Not funny, Mr. Coordinated," Mindy snorted. "Remember who's always falling."

"Try to stay in the center of the logs," Miguel instructed. "I'm sure you've done this when you were kids, but probably not so far. If you do fall, try to get up smoothly, without a lot of jerking."

Everyone took a deep breath. Jeff followed closely behind Miguel. He couldn't walk very fast because staying balanced required all his concentration. The logs were slippery and unstable. It reminded him of log rolling contests he'd seen on television.

When they were about halfway across, Jeff heard a big splash behind him. He couldn't turn fast for fear of losing his balance. Carefully stepping to the next log, he looked back.

K.J. was up to his waist in the mud. He frantically clawed at the logs to keep from sinking deeper. His backpack was holding him down. He looked desperate, but he couldn't speak.

Miguel headed toward K.J. as Jeff, Mindy, and Warren watched in horror, afraid to move.

"Hold on, K.J. I'll get you out of there," Miguel called.

K.J. struggled harder, and Jeff knew they'd never find him if he sunk. Mindy stood frozen with fear. Warren tried to cheer K.J. on.

K.J. worked frantically. Clawing, slipping back, clawing harder, slipping again. Miguel moved as close as he could, but he was still too far away to get to K.J.

"If I try to help," Miguel told K.J., "my weight will pull us both in."

Jeff saw a frightened look on K.J.'s face. Deeper and deeper he went. *This must be what quicksand is like*, Jeff thought. He prayed.

Miguel stopped in front of K.J. and looked him in the eyes. "First, try to relax."

K.J. nodded.

"Now lift yourself up...slowly," Miguel continued calmly.

Miraculously, K.J. began to come up. With Miguel coaching him, he slowly climbed up on a larger log. He crouched there for a moment, catching his breath. Trembling and breathing hard, he looked up at the others.

"Oh man," he said slowly. "I don't know about this Amazon missionary work."

K.J.'s pants were caked with thick, black mud. The rest of his body was wet, and his head was splattered with the muck.

Mindy giggled. "Wish I had a camera."

K.J. looked at her and scowled. "Good thing my camera is in a waterproof bag. But with any luck Mindy, you could be next."

After K.J. had a rest, the team continued across. Concentrating on each step, they prayed quietly as they moved from log to log to log. No one bothered to talk.

Perspiration rolled down Jeff's face. Finally, he saw dry ground on the other side of the marsh. He wanted to scream, but he knew it would make everyone lose focus.

One by one, they stepped off the logs and onto the jungle floor. K.J. fell to the ground, exhausted. Jeff knew his buddy liked adventure, but K.J. had probably reached his limit.

After a short rest, Warren looked at his watch. "It's almost five. If we go now, we'll get to the camp in time for dinner."

"Sounds good to me," Mindy said.

"A shower sounds good to me," K.J. muttered. "And a washer and dryer."

Warren laughed. "The washers and dryers are different out here. They're not coin operated."

Jeff laughed out loud. "And you can't plug your hair dryer into a tree."

Everyone laughed as the team moved on. Suddenly, Mindy screamed and fell to the ground.

"What's wrong?" Jeff asked, as he ran to his sister.

"I tripped over a tree root. I think I sprained my ankle," she said, rubbing it.

Jeff groaned. "I'll sure be glad to get there."

Jeff carefully removed her muddy tennis shoe and looked at her ankle. Warren and Miguel joined him.

"Looks like it's swelling a little," Jeff said, retying her shoe.

"Do you think you can make it another ten minutes?" Miguel asked.

"I don't know," Mindy grimaced. "I'll try."

Mindy struggled to her feet. She hobbled along, trying to be brave. Then she stopped. "How about making me a crutch out of a stick?"

Miguel found a stick with a twisted knot on the top. "Try this, Mindy. It isn't far now."

Jeff stopped everyone. "We need to pray for her. God can heal her. This place is known for sickness." Jeff placed his hand on Mindy's foot and prayed.

After Jeff's amen, Mindy tried to get up. "I'll be okay," she said after a few steps with the crutch.

"I'm proud of you," K.J. said, smiling. "You're quite a trooper. Hand me your backpack. I'll carry it for you."

Mindy smiled, handing it to K.J.

The tired team made their way slowly toward the village. It was hot. They were hungry. And their clothes were torn from trees and vines along the way.

Suddenly, Jeff heard the strangest noise.

Chapter 6

Higher Ground

What's that?" Mindy cried.

Miguel laughed. "I know you've had a hard day. But you can relax now. That's the sound of the village. It's the way the Indians communicate with each other."

Jeff let out a sigh of relief.

"Listen." Miguel motioned everyone to be still.

"Ooooooooooooooooooh. Oooooooooooooooh."

Jeff was tempted to laugh.

"Oooooooooooooooooooooooooooooooooh," the sound came back.

"Hey! They're talking to us," K.J. yelled. "I can't believe we're finally here!"

As they rounded a curve in the path, Jeff got his first glimpse of the village which was to be home for a while. A dozen or so palm-roofed houses were scattered around a central open area. The rectangular houses were made of bamboo and other woods from the jungle.

The red earth along the village paths was a striking contrast to the solid green backdrop. The tangled vines formed a living wall on every side, as though waiting patiently to take over.

A host of brown-skinned Indian men appeared from out of the houses. Children peeked from behind trees, each wearing a big grin. Jeff, Mindy, K.J., and Warren grinned back.

There were about two hundred Jarawaras. This village, called Aquabranca, was only one of their six villages. The men, who averaged about 5'3", had either dark brown or black hair. Some of them had slight red highlights in their coloring.

"Hey, this is great," K.J. whispered to Jeff. "I feel tall around here."

Jeff nudged his buddy in the ribs while he studied the villagers closely. Most had full, round eyes, while a few had eyes which looked a little slanted because of a heavy fold of skin under their eyebrows. Some were nice-looking. Others had faces that were different than Jeff was used to seeing.

The men were dressed in shorts and T-shirts. Jeff knew that wasn't always the case. When they had first talked of coming here, Mindy had been nervous. She thought she'd be embarrassed because the men wore hardly anything except a G-string, but additional research had shown her that the

Jarawaras had adjusted to being in contact with the Brazilian culture.

The Jarawara men looked the team over for a few minutes. Jeff laughed, thinking how funny they must have looked to the Jarawara—Mindy hobbling and leaning on a stick, K.J. filthy with black mud, and everybody else sweaty, dirty, and torn. But he hadn't thought of the other things that were strange to the Jarawara.

The children had never seen blonde hair. Jeff's was dishwater blond and short, so he didn't get too much attention. But Mindy's hair was the color of honey. It fell long and straight from her ponytail.

Giggling, the children inched out from behind the trees to get a better look. On a bough above her, one little girl reached out a finger to touch it. Dozens of little ones gathered around.

Mindy smiled, pulled out the ponytail band, and ran her fingers through her hair. When she bent over and shook her hair playfully, the kids jumped up and down and clapped their hands. With everyone laughing, Miguel lead them to the center of the village.

From a house at the far end, an older gentleman hurried out to meet them. He was nearly six feet tall and had dark hair which had grayed at the temples. His friendly face was wrinkled from years in the sun. He wore a faded safari suit with torn canvas shoes. He hugged Miguel, then he turned to Warren.

"I'm happy to finally meet you, Dr. Jones," Warren said, stepping forward.

As Warren introduced each member of the team, Jeff felt instant admiration for this medical doctor who had lived among the Jarawara for fifteen years.

Jeff remembered hearing that Dr. Jones's wife had died of a tropical disease in the village four years earlier. Dr. Jones had sacrificed a lot to live among strangers in the middle of the Amazon, Jeff realized. No electricity, no family, none of the comforts of being home. It was a sacrifice of love.

Dr. Jones introduced a very tall Jarawara man with a boy. "This is Chief Naati and She'a, his son."

Everyone shook hands, smiling and laughing as they toured the village. Jeff looked around, not believing he was actually there. He felt like he had stepped back in time, away from the noises of twentieth century. There were no roads, no cars, no phones, no noise or pollution.

Jeff saw women laughing among themselves. In a thatched, covered area that reminded him of the barbecue area of a park, they chopped vegetables and stirred pots. The smell of meat filled the air, making his mouth water.

Dressed in T-shirts and brightly printed wrap-around skirts, the women were short and stocky like the men. Miguel told them the Jarawara fiercely protected their women. They were afraid of disease, rape, and evil spirits, so they kept their wives away from outsiders.

Over to one side, Jeff spotted what had to be Dr. Jones's house. The building was a little larger than the others. A thatched roof created a porch out front. Through the window, he saw tables and medical supplies. Jeff guessed Dr. Jones lived behind the clinic.

Then Jeff walked over to a cage made of bamboo. Mindy and K.J. were already there. A light brown monkey peeked out at them. He looked up at Jeff with curious eyes, then jumped onto a perch, wrapping his long tail all the way around his body. He was obviously someone's pet.

As the tribe went about their daily routine, Jeff wished he could communicate with them. He wanted to know these people and share the love of Jesus with them. Watching Mindy and K.J. play with the kids told him they felt the same way.

A Jarawara man and Miguel showed the team where they would sleep. The guys stayed with the single Indian men. Inside their building, hammocks hung every which way. Some of them were so near the ceiling that Jeff wondered how anyone got in or out of them without killing himself.

Mindy was staying with a family of girls. Before dinner, she sat on the family's porch step while three little girls took turns brushing her hair.

Jeff realized how hungry he was as they came to the eating area. Chief Naati was there, smiling at them.

Miguel moved closer to Jeff. "I'll bet you guys are ready to eat after today."

"You can say that again." Jeff laughed. "It smells terrific. What do the Jarawara eat?"

Miguel grinned. "Mostly fish and bread. My favorite thing is a bread crumb dish they make out of sweet potatoes. They somehow toast it over the fire until it's real crispy."

"Sounds good to me," Jeff replied.

"And they eat fruit—pineapples, bananas, lemons, guava. Whatever grows in the jungle. That's why they aren't very big. They live on fish and fruits."

K.J. walked over. "So what's for dinner?"

"Fish and fruit." Miguel laughed.

Someone handed Jeff a plate and a fork. "Hey! I thought everything was primitive out here. I didn't know you had forks."

Dr. Jones laughed. He turned to Chief Naati, who was eating with his hands, and explained what Jeff had said. They laughed.

"Obviously," Jeff said shaking his head at the fork, "you brought a few customs with you from Iowa."

Soon everyone was laughing. Jeff saw the kindness Dr. Jones had for the Indians, and he knew they were one big family.

Dr. Jones put down his food and smiled at the club. "I'm so glad you're here. I want to make your stay the best possible."

"Well, today was kinda rough," Jeff said, "but this is turning out to be the best experience of my life. I know I'll never be the same after seeing your commitment to these people."

"Aaaah, they're great people," the doctor said humbly. "I'm sorry about your equipment being confiscated. But I've got a plane scheduled to take Chief Naati and I into Labrea Wednesday because we must go to court. I was lucky to get a plane."

"You're not kidding," Mindy said.

Dr. Jones grinned again. "I've asked Warren to go with me. We'll try to get your equipment back."

K.J. stopped between bites of fish. "I can't believe those guys took it! Warren worked months to get permission—and on paper too."

"I understand," Dr. Jones said. "In all the years

I've been here, this is probably the most crucial time for you to videotape the tribe."

"Why's that?" Mindy asked.

"There's a battle raging over land ownership. Some of the wealthy landowners want to control everything. They're trying to get rid of tribal people."

"How can they do that? The Indians have been here longer, haven't they?" Jeff asked.

"It's a long story, Jeff. I'll tell you more tomorrow." Dr. Jones smiled. "I know how tired you must be."

"It has been a long day," Jeff admitted. "I can't wait to hear all the details, though."

"Tomrrow," Dr. Jones said. "I'll tell you everything tomorrow."

Jeff settled back to finish his meal. The fruit was delicious, and he couldn't get enough bread crumbs. Mindy and K.J. had taken off to play tag with the kids. They were having a blast, even if Mindy still hobbled slightly. Both K.J. and Mindy had forgotten the terrible journey and already fit into the tribe.

Watching Warren talk to Dr. Jones and the chief, Jeff was thankful for the man who made these trips possible. He knew he could be home, riding his mountain bike or watching a movie. But no movie could compare to the real world and the real people he met while he was doing God's work. Because of his experiences with the Reel Kids Club, his life had meaning.

The campfire was reflected in the eyes of the Jarawara Indians. Jeff saw curiosity there. They were a unique and special people God had created.

Dr. Jones turned to Jeff again. "I know you're

tired, but Warren mentioned you might like to share a greeting with the tribe."

Jeff couldn't believe his ears. He had wanted to speak to the Jarawara from the moment he arrived. But now butterflies took flight in his stomach and his mind went blank. "Sure," he said anyway.

Jeff listened as Dr. Jones explained to Chief Naati what was going to happen. The chief grinned at Jeff as he stood up. He said a few things to his tribe. They laughed.

Dr. Jones translated for Jeff. "He told them you came a long ways to share with us. I'll translate for you."

Jeff's mind was still blank as he stood to face the crowd. He didn't want to say the wrong thing and mess up fifteen years of hard work.

Forty pairs of dark eyes fixed on him. He whispered a quick prayer and began. "We've come from America to spend the next few days with you."

Jeff waited for the translation.

"It's a joy to meet you. We hope to learn your ways. Dr. Jones has told us how special you are. The world would not be complete without you.

"We want to learn of your culture. We also want to help Dr. Jones in any way we can."

The glistening eyes Jeff saw in the group were different than the stranger's in the canoe. Jeff hoped he had connected with their hearts.

"We'd like to take some pictures to share the story of your tribe with others. You have made us feel at home. If we do some awkward things, please try to understand. Thank you for your hospitality."

Dr. Jones finished translating, and Jeff sat down. Chief Naati took his place and began to speak.

"We're happy your club is here," Dr. Jones interpreted the chief's words. "Dr. Jones has been talking about your coming for months. We've looked forward to this time. Please be yourselves and feel at home with us.

"Dr. Jones means much to us. He's cared for our wives, delivered our children, and taught us much about life. We are grateful to him for trying to protect our future."

Dr. Jones looked embarrassed translating words that praised him. Tears appeared in his eyes, and he smiled at Chief Naati.

"We want to help you with your film project. We will show you our way of life. But we know you are tired. We hope you have a good rest."

Dr. Jones finished, nodding at the last line.

Jeff looked at Miguel, who sat next to him, then scanned the crowd. All the Indians were smiling at him—except one. Jeff noticed a blank stare on one man. He thought it might be an angry stare.

Jeff turned cautiously to Miguel. "That man doesn't look too happy. Have I done something to upset him?"

"Probably not," Miguel whispered back. "He's the village shaman."

Chapter 7

The Medicine Man

Jeff wasn't sure he wanted to know what Miguel meant. "What's a shaman?"

"He's the spiritual leader," Miguel whispered to Jeff. "Every Indian village in South America has its shaman."

"Like a witch doctor? We once had all kinds of trouble with a witch doctor in Kenya."

"Sort of. He's looked at as their religious leader. He's not too happy that so many Christians are here at once."

"Why?" Jeff asked as Mindy joined them again.

Miguel smiled. "Because you're a threat to him.

If the village believes in Dr. Jones's teaching, it means the shaman is out of a job."

Jeff pursed his lips. He slowly took a breath. "Never a dull minute around here, is there?"

Miguel laughed. "Not for you guys."

Mindy rolled her eyes. "I think we're too tired to handle anything tonight. I need to hit the sack."

Miguel laughed. "You mean the hammock."

❖❖❖❖❖❖❖

Jeff awoke as tropical sunlight flooded through the thatched roof. His stomach was slightly nauseous because of the swaying hammock. With mosquito netting over him as well as under him, he felt like a moth ready to kick its way out of a cocoon.

Near him, Warren and K.J. were sprawled in their hammocks. K.J. was snoring loudly. Warren slowly stretched.

Jeff's thoughts turned to Scripture passages he had studied for the trip. They were all about tribes. Jesus was from the tribe of Judah. Other passages spoke about how every kindred, tribe, and tongue would take their place in heaven. People from every part of mankind would be there.

Jeff realized again how important the Jarawaras were to God. The heavenly Father didn't want anyone missing. Jesus made that clear when He said to go into all the world and preach the good news. That meant even the most remote jungles.

Jeff tried to picture the heavenly scene. He could see Chief Naati and his tribe sitting around God's throne with Jesus. That could never happen without a Dr. Jones.

Warren tried to climb out of his hammock. Jeff laughed while he struggled to get his feet on the ground.

Warren yawned, chuckling to himself. "This isn't as easy as it looks. But I sure slept well. Did you?"

Jeff nodded. "Warren, I'm really glad you started this club. I hope more people start clubs like this. I can't believe how important missionaries and Bible translators are. God's been showing me how important every tribe is to Him."

Warren smiled his approval. "There are hundreds of tribes like this who have never heard of Jesus."

"Yeah," Jeff pondered. "But God wants every tribe around His throne. How many more people do you think are needed to tell them?"

"Hundreds, maybe thousands," Warren said, pulling on his shirt. "One missionary said, 'I see the smoke of a thousand villages.' It was a vision—the way God told him he was to reach many tribes."

"If these tribes don't hear about Jesus, then their only hope is in their witch doctors or shamans."

"I guess you saw him last night," Warren said.

"Yeah. He didn't look very happy."

"That's okay," Warren replied. "Dr. Jones told me that even the shaman can't deny the miracles he's seen. We'll pray for him too."

"Sounds good to me."

K.J. opened his eyes, groaned, and rolled over. "Do you think they'll give our equipment back? I feel naked without my camcorder."

Smiling, Warren nodded. "Dr. Jones says he knows people in Labrea who will cut through the red tape."

Jeff yawned. "What's our schedule like this week, Warren?"

"Dr. Jones wants to talk to us this morning. Later we'll help him in his clinic. It's open Tuesdays and Fridays."

"Is it just for the Jarawara?" K.J. asked.

"No," Warren answered. "Poor Brazilians often take the same trip we took yesterday to get medical help. For some reason, there's a lot of sickness in this area."

"What about the rest of the week?" Jeff wanted to know.

"Chief Naati wants you to have fun. He's planned a fishing trip on Thursday. The rest of the time can be spent learning about the tribe. I'll be going with Dr. Jones into Labrea tomorrow."

"Am I going with you?" K.J. asked.

"Maybe it's best if you stay here. Dr. Jones said you'll have time to get all the footage you need. There are rivers and streams all over the area. And you can do some filming from the plane on our way home."

"Sounds good. I'm not goin' over any more logs!"

"Yeah," Warren said. "We should be able to fly in and out of Labrea in one day. That'll save a lot of time."

"And a lot of muck," K.J. said with a chuckle.

❖ ❖ ❖ ❖ ❖ ❖ ❖

After bananas and guavas for breakfast, the boys headed for Dr. Jones's house. Like the others, it was built on stilts.

Jeff checked his watch. It was 10:30. Inside Dr. Jones's, he looked around. A kerosene lamp and a jar of pencils decorated an old desk. A stack of mail sat in the center of it. A dark haired woman with a dazzling smile gazed at him from a photo on the wall. Jeff thought it must be the doctor's deceased wife.

Mats covered the dirt floor. Jeff saw medical supplies stacked along the back wall. Mosquito netting was draped over two traditional beds in the corner.

Sheets hanging from the ceiling created examination rooms. Chairs were scattered about. Jeff sensed this room was often a beehive of activity.

Mindy's crutch tapped up the stairs, but she was hardly using it this morning. Dr. Jones offered padded wooden chairs to sit on.

"Let me tell you what's going on so you can pray," Dr. Jones said seriously.

Everybody leaned forward.

Relaxing in his chair, Dr. Jones scratched his head. "We have to go to court tomorrow. A greedy landowner is trying to get control of all the land in this area. He wants to enslave the Jarawara people. The man is from England. His family has owned land here since the early 1900s."

Jeff couldn't hold back. As if he were in school, he raised his hand. "Is this man Mr. Giles?"

Dr. Jones nodded but looked sad. "Yes. Warren told me you met him at the airport."

"So that's why he became cold when we mentioned your name!" Jeff put the pieces of the puzzle together.

Mindy turned to Dr. Jones. "Why is he trying to take Indian land?"

Dr. Jones shook his head. "Mr. Giles doesn't know much about life here. He's only here for the court hearing. Because he's lived in England most of his life, he's a total stranger to the Amazon. Brazilian natives manage his property."

Jeff smiled. "I think we met one of them on the canoe yesterday."

K.J.'s face flushed with anger. "Why doesn't this guy stick to his own property?"

"It's a long story," Dr. Jones said.

"Please tell us," Mindy pleaded softly.

"I'll make it brief," Dr. Jones said. "In the early 1900s, there was a big demand for latex rubber. Rubber trees grow in the highlands where the Indians live. The demand for rubber brought the first contact between the Jarawara and the native Brazilians and Indians from other tribes."

Everyone sat on the edge of their seats, waiting to hear more.

"Brazilians claimed as much land as they could see," Dr. Jones continued. "Mr. Giles's father bought the rights to the land from the Brazilians. He divided it between his six sons."

"So Mr. Giles inherited it," Jeff concluded.

"Exactly. The bottom fell out of rubber prices in 1912. When that happened, the land was useless to the family. But after World War II, they began selling the wood from the rain forest. It's very valuable."

"What kind of wood?" Jeff asked.

"Mahogany, monkeypot—hard, expensive woods. They grow near the rubber trees. They've been fighting to control the land ever since."

K.J. got up. "Why can't he buy the wood from the Indians?"

"Good question, K.J.," Dr. Jones responded. "The landowners have never recognized the Indians' right to live here. They want them out. Usually they just take the trees they want. Sometimes, they pay the Indians for their labor, but it's not a fair price."

"Why don't the Indians fight back?" Mindy asked.

"Three reasons. They feel powerless against the big logging equipment the landowners bring in. They don't read and write, so they're easily intimidated. And they don't speak Portuguese or understand the legal system."

"Wow," Jeff said. "They must feel pretty helpless."

Dr. Jones sat back. "This is where I come in. For years, I've tried to help them get the land legally divided. The highlands have been their home for centuries—the Indians are entitled to it. But the owners' political power is strong."

"So Mr. Giles is trying to win control of the land and the trees in court tomorrow?" Jeff asked.

"Right." Dr. Jones nodded.

"Do the Indian people have a chance?" Mindy's eyes were wide with concern.

"Yes. That's why your visit is so important. For years, I've tried to get the courts to recognize the Indians. Just your being here, especially with your cameras, puts pressure on the leaders to make a decision."

"It must be important if Mr. Giles came all the way from England," K.J. added thoughtfully.

"You're right. He doesn't care about the land or the Indians. He cares about the money he makes

Chapter 8

Fire!

Yes," Dr. Jones said sadly. "It's not just lumber they want, but oil, gold, and development. Unfortunately, the bulldozers and logging machinery they bring in are destroying the rain forest and everything in it. It's the tribes who suffer."

"Can't somebody stop it?" Mindy cried.

"We can't turn back time," Dr. Jones replied. "I believe in progress, but we need to be sensitive to the world around us. Plants, animals, and even the people who live in the jungle are disappearing fast."

"It sounds like the developers will wipe out anybody who gets in their way," Jeff said.

"Now you see why Mr. Giles got angry when he found out you were visiting me. Especially this week."

"Wow," Mindy said. "I didn't realize this was such an important issue."

"If he wins, we'll hear his bulldozers and chainsaws the following day," Dr. Jones said. "He wants a fight."

Jeff looked at his watch. It was almost time for lunch.

Dr. Jones smiled. "I'll bet you guys are hungry."

"We're teenagers." K.J. laughed. "We're always hungry."

"The Indians don't eat lunch," Dr. Jones said. "And if they don't have any leftovers from dinner, they don't have breakfast."

Mindy's face looked worried. "Fish for breakfast?"

"Don't worry, Mindy," Dr. Jones said, getting up. "I've stockpiled a few things for you guys."

❖❖❖❖❖❖❖

After they ate, Jeff, K.J., and Mindy unloaded some of the medical supplies the men had picked up from the canoe landing. The team helped Dr. Jones prepare for the clinic.

Mindy wiped off a table. "Can I ask you a question, Dr. Jones?"

"Sure."

"Have you seen many people come to Jesus?"

Dr. Jones stopped and looked at her. "This may shock you, but in fifteen years I haven't seen a single convert. But I've translated a good part of the Bible, and the Jarawara understand what I believe."

"Nobody has come to Jesus? Why?"

"Tribes make decisions together. If they do decide to follow Jesus, everybody will."

"Wow," Mindy responded. "That's exciting. Can I ask one more question? What do people do all day? They don't go to school or work, do they?"

"Well, the Jarawara are a very hard-working people. They get up early and go to bed early. The men hunt, fish, and work on their houses. The women gather and prepare food, raise their children, and make things like baskets or necklaces."

"Sounds like us—except for the cars and noise."

"That's right." Dr. Jones looked at his watch. "It's almost two. The clinic opens in a half hour. People will start arriving soon."

"What kind of medical help do you give?" Mindy asked.

"Cuts, bruises, an occasional broken bone. But mostly I treat tropical diseases. People say if you want to study tropical disease, this is the perfect place. We have every kind here. Years ago, the Peru Peru Indians named this area `Maciari Maci.' It means, `Falling down sick.' "

"Falling down sick?" Mindy questioned.

"There's a curse on this region. To do health care is to do spiritual warfare. This place has yellow fever, measles, chicken pox, malaria, hepatitis— every kind of tropical fever you can imagine. We have skin diseases not found anywhere else in the world."

"Have you had success in helping these people?"

"Not like I want. I'd love to have more prayer cover focused on this part of the world. Maybe you could ask your friends at home to pray for the work here."

Jeff had heard every word. At that moment, two Brazilian men shyly approached. Their shabby clothes told him they were very poor. One man looked like he had a serious skin disease.

Dr. Jones asked them to sit down, then gathered the team together. "Let's have some prayer. Then you guys can handle the cuts and bruises by cleaning them and applying disinfectant and bandages. Don't forget to wash your hands very carefully and often. We don't want to spread disease among the Jarawara people."

Everyone nodded. Mindy passed the surgical soap around. She was bouncing with excitement because she had taken some medical courses in preparation for this trip.

Dr. Jones bowed his head. "Lord, help us to be Your hands and heart to these hurting people. May they know Your healing touch."

Everyone said an amen.

Jeff squeezed the doctor's hand. "Lord," Jeff prayed, "we take authority against this `sickness curse.' You died so people could be healed. You rose again to give us power over demons, sickness, and even death."

Jeff felt a strong confidence rising in his spirit as he prayed. He had never felt like this before.

Everyone lifted their heads. Jeff looked outside. He couldn't believe his eyes. A long line of people had formed in front of the clinic. Jeff saw a mixture of Indians and native Brazilians. A few mothers held babies that looked very sick. With no clocks, he wondered how they knew it was time for the clinic to open.

Dr. Jones moved quickly through the people, dividing them into two lines. He would handle the serious cases. Mindy and the team would handle the rest.

Even the sick children wanted to stay in Mindy's line so they could touch her blonde hair. All afternoon, she was the most popular person there. K.J. snapped photos from every angle.

"This is what it's all about," Mindy said as she bandaged cuts and soothed fretful children. She prayed for each one. "I can't help thinking how much Jesus loves every one of these children."

❖❖❖❖❖❖❖

Later that evening Dr. Jones and the team sat down for a delicious dinner of fish and fruit.

"Tell us more about the battle over the trees, Dr. Jones," Jeff said. "Why do the Indians allow them to take the wood if it's theirs?"

"Nobody, including the courts, has the courage to say whose land it is. Everybody knows it's Indian land, but the landowners pay the courts off."

Mindy raised her eyebrows. "Miguel said wood is the most sought after product in the Amazon."

K.J. scratched his head. "How do they get it out of here? They sure can't carry huge trees out on their backs—especially tiptoeing over the marsh we came through yesterday!"

"During the rainy season, the water rises. It gets very close to the villages. The traders give the Indians chainsaws to cut the wood. Then they float it out of the inlet to the Perus River and down the Amazon River."

Mindy's face turned beet red. "You mean they have the Indians cut the wood they're stealing from them?"

"I'm afraid so. River traders and landowners keep the Indians in debt. That way Mr. Giles and his men enslave them."

"I don't understand," K.J. said.

"Education equals power," Dr. Jones explained. "The Indians don't have either. Since they can't read, write, or do math, the Brazilians cheat them out of fair prices. Then they give them alcohol and drugs to control them."

"I don't believe this!" Jeff said, pounding his hand on the table.

"That's why they don't want people like me and you coming in to educate the Indians. Education puts them on equal ground with the traders, and they don't like it. Mr. Giles's father thought he owned the Jarawara tribe. But tomorrow, that's going to change."

Dr. Jones looked concerned as he continued. "It's war. Chief Naati told me there was a fight today between Mr. Giles's men and his. Fortunately, no one was hurt. But the Indians need to stand up for their rights. It's all coming to a head."

Warren stood up. "We need a good night's sleep. We have a busy day tomorrow."

K.J. yawned, causing a chain reaction.

Jeff stood up, heading for the house. "I don't know about you guys, but I'm tired. I'm going to bed."

"Me too," Mindy said.

❖ ❖ ❖ ❖ ❖ ❖

Jeff kept rocking his hammock, not able to get his mind off the landowners' unfair practices. They had no regard for the beauty of the Indian culture. He finally fell asleep praying about it.

Suddenly, Jeff was awakened by a loud noise. Jumping clumsily out of his hammock, he ran outside. Warren and K.J. were right beside him.

A bright light lit up the whole village. With eyes open in disbelief, Jeff turned to the others.

"The medical clinic's on fire!"

Chapter 9

Falling Sick

Jeff's sleepy eyes popped open. Dr. Jones was shouting instructions as he beat back the flames with a blanket. A number of Jarawaras carried handmade wooden buckets back and forth to a nearby stream.

Miguel came running, and Jeff rushed over. "What's the doctor saying?"

"Save the medical supplies!" Miguel yelled.

The flames had already gobbled up the clinic's thatched roof. As Jeff watched, the front porch collapsed with a mighty *whoosh*. He hoped the whole village wouldn't burn down.

Suddenly, he heard explosions. Balls of fire burst

into the air. Jeff knew the chemicals from the medical supplies were igniting. Feeling helpless, he stood there, not knowing whether to help beat out the flames or stay away from the explosions.

Mindy herded the children away from the fire. K.J. was shooting pictures. Warren ran to help Dr. Jones fight the flames.

Jeff turned to Miguel in frustration. "Is there anything we can do?"

"It's too hot in there," Miguel replied. "Those chemicals are too dangerous."

Jeff wanted to do something, but he knew the fire was beyond his control. "What about the men?"

"Dr. Jones won't let them get hurt."

Dr. Jones began yelling to the Indians as he waved them away from the fire. Squinting, Jeff saw several boxes of medical supplies that hadn't been unpacked sitting just a few yards from the burning building. Jeff nodded to Miguel, and they were off. K.J. knew what they were going to do, and he followed with his camera.

Running to within five or six feet of the raging flames, they snatched up as many supplies as they could carry. They set them under a tree a safe distance away and rushed back for more.

"Be careful, you guys," Warren called.

Just as he spoke, there was another explosion. Jeff felt the heat on his face. He jumped back and fell to the ground. Miguel and K.J. lay alongside him.

Dr. Jones ran over and scooted them all to safety. "Get back! We can't save anything else."

Everyone took a few steps back. Jeff stood there with the others, watching helplessly as the fire consumed the rest of the clinic. The men had doused the adjoining huts with enough water to protect them, but the clinic burned quickly and completely.

The explosions finally stopped, and the fire died down. The Jarawara men poured bucket after bucket of water over the hot embers. There was a sadness in Dr. Jones's eyes as he poked through the ashes with a stick. Years of work had gone up in smoke. The clinic and most of the doctor's supplies had been destroyed.

Dr. Jones collapsed on a tree stump, and Warren quietly joined him. The Jarawara men stood helplessly by. Chief Naati sat a few feet away. No one said a word.

Jeff wondered if it had been an accident or an evil attack.

After a few minutes, Dr. Jones spoke. "I know who did this. A women who was here with her baby saw two Brazilians running into the jungle. It had to be Mr. Giles's men. It's obvious he will stop at nothing to win. Nothing."

The Wednesday morning light came sooner than Jeff wanted. No one had gotten back to bed until well after two o'clock. After they made sure the fire was out, the men had taken turns guarding the village.

Today was the day Dr. Jones and Warren were going to court in Labrea where they would have to face Mr. Giles. Jeff looked around. K.J. was still asleep, but Warren's hammock was already empty. Walking to the porch, Jeff looked toward the clinic. He rubbed his eyes in disbelief.

The Jarawara men had already cleared the rubble away. Women carried large baskets of ashes and burnt wood. Dr. Jones, Miguel, and Warren were going through the remaining medical supplies, saving anything they could.

Pulling on his shoes, Jeff ran out to help. "I can't believe how fast you're cleaning up!"

Warren smiled, his face streaked with black marks. "The Jarawara are going to build a new clinic today. They are tired of the attacks. This fire may be the thing that gives them the courage to stand up against Mr. Giles."

Jeff was speechless but excited.

Warren held up a box of bandages. "A lot of stuff was saved. Today, you guys can help the men build the new clinic. It'll be fun." He smiled. "The plane will be here to pick Dr. Jones and me up in an hour. Think I'll get cleaned up first."

Jeff wiped his eyes. "Where's the airstrip?"

"That way," Warren said, pointing into the jungle. "The Jarawara built it for Dr. Jones five years ago."

"Whose plane is it?" Jeff wanted to know.

"It belongs to Mission Flyers Fellowship. It was being repaired a couple of days ago, or they would have picked us up in Labrea when we came in."

"That would have been nice." Jeff laughed.

"Get something to eat, then you can start building."

"Great!" Jeff was excited. "This is what we came for."

❖❖❖❖❖❖❖

When they heard a plane overhead, the whole village ran toward the runway to see Dr. Jones and Warren off. The strip was cut out of the jungle and was just long enough for a small plane to take off and land.

By the time the crowd arrived, the MFF pilot had landed the Cessna 206 and had it ready to go again. Chief Naati stood with arm around his son's shoulders. Warren said goodbye to the team. Dr. Jones spoke to the tribe. In one big circle, everyone joined hands and bowed their heads to pray for the judge to rule in their favor.

Nearly everyone, Jeff noticed, except the shaman, who still looked angry. Then the passengers climbed aboard, and the plane took off.

❖❖❖❖❖❖❖

When everyone got back to the village, someone gave Mindy and K.J. machetes. At first, using the large knives was difficult, so they were slow and careful. But soon they were trimming the bark off logs like experts.

Nine-foot crotched poles held cross pieces to support the thatched roof. For the walls, Miguel and the Jarawara men used long vertical poles, planted close together. These were held in place with horizontal strips of bamboo, forming the skeleton of the house. Women gathered stacks of palm leaves and tied them together to form the roof.

Everyone worked diligently. Jeff saw She'a, the chief's son, busy cutting bamboo. No one, not even K.J., stopped to eat. Everyone was excited to get the job done.

Jeff began to understand the affection the Jarawara people had for Dr. Jones and his work. The villagers laughed and smiled as they worked side by side.

Mindy had put down her machete and was helping the women weave bamboo poles together with palm fronds. Jeff took over trimming bark so K.J. could take a few photos.

"This fire is turning out to be a blessing," Jeff remarked.

K.J. snapped the shutter. "Yeah. This clinic will be twice as big. I've never seen anything go up so fast. But I hope Mr. Giles doesn't send any more visitors."

Jeff nodded as he cut away a chunk of bark. "Well, if he loses his case in court, it may end his tricks. But this is giving the people courage and uniting them. They've got to win that case today."

Mindy walked over, brushing damp hair out of her eyes. She looked tired. "Whew. This is fun, but I don't know if I could live in one of these huts for long."

One of the Jarawara men brought over some halved coconut shells containing cold drinks.

"I wonder what it is." Mindy looked at the liquid closely.

"Taste it and see," K.J. challenged.

Mindy slowly put it to her mouth. "Mmmm. Delicious. It's like a fruit punch. Try some."

Jeff and K.J. stopped what they were doing and drank until the punch was gone.

"Ah, this is the life." K.J. sighed, leaning against a tree. "You know, I'm really impressed with all the tools the Indians make out of coconut shells. We ought to take some of these home with us."

"Yeah," Jeff said. "They could easily replace cereal bowls. And they'd make great bike helmets for babies," he added, putting the empty shell on his head.

Mindy laughed out loud. K.J. snapped a picture.

Jeff looked at the other tools the Jarawara were using. Most were as modern as the ones used in America. He saw axes, saws, hammers, nails, wheelbarrows, and even a few gas-powered tools. He guessed the villagers had gotten them from the river traders.

Jeff watched the women weaving. Chairs and baskets were quickly taking shape.

K.J. turned to Jeff. "It's too bad there are evil men like Mr. Giles in the world."

"Mr. Giles probably thinks what he's doing is right," Jeff said thoughtfully. "He doesn't care about the Indians. He wants them off the land—even if he has to burn them out."

Miguel walked up, wiping sweat from his forehead.

"Hey, Miguel," Jeff greeted their new friend. "Has Mr. Giles used fire as a weapon before?"

Miguel frowned. "No. Not fire. Up until now, he didn't need to. The Jarawara did whatever he wanted."

Jeff thought for a moment about the situation. "You're a native Brazilian, Miguel," he finally said. "Who do you think has the rights to the land?"

Miguel rubbed his square jaw. "My opinion doesn't really count. I like these people. Tribes were here before many of us. I believe it's their land. The landowners and traders should treat them with respect. But the problem is that the Indians are on the land that is valuable for wood and other things."

"Yeah. I see how that creates a problem," Jeff said.

Suddenly, a cry came from near the side of a house. Jeff saw some women leaning over a child. The child was groaning, doubled up in pain.

Jeff and Mindy quickly ran over.

"It's She'a!" Jeff cried.

Chapter 10

The Shaman

Everyone gathered around She'a. His eyes were rolled back, and he was breathing slowly.

"What's wrong?" Mindy whispered.

Jeff looked at Mindy and K.J. "We need to pray and break this curse."

Before they had a chance, though, the shaman appeared, scooped the boy up in his arms, and carried him to his house.

Jeff ran to Miguel. "What's he doing?"

Miguel shook his head. "This is very normal, Jeff. The shaman is expected to heal She'a. Every tribe takes their sick to the shaman for healing. It makes me glad I'm Brazilian."

"What will he do?" Mindy cried.

"He may crush leaves from some tree to make a potion."

"Potion?"

"A drug. He'll get high and probably see strange things."

"What will that do for She'a?" Mindy demanded.

"Look, you guys," Miguel said. "I'm out of my league here. You'll have to ask Dr. Jones about the fine print. But I believe the shaman is possessed by the devil to do his work."

Mindy's eyes almost popped out. She became angry. "He's working with the devil to heal She'a?"

"That's right," Miguel said. "The Indians are frightened of spirits. That's why they respect the jungle and don't go out at night. They believe there are spirits all around."

Everyone listened carefully as Miguel went on. "They believe their village is a safe haven from the spirits. They think sickness comes when someone displeases the spirits."

"I'll bet the shaman thinks we're the ones displeasing the spirits," Jeff pointed out.

"You're probably right." Miguel nodded his head. "But if it makes you feel any better, I don't think he's nuts about me either." Miguel sighed. "The Indians are so paranoid that if someone dies, they usually move the village. That's why the tribes move around a lot."

Jeff snapped his fingers, getting new understanding. "That explains how the landowners can take advantage of them! If they keep moving, they can't lay claim to a certain piece of land."

"Exactly," Miguel said.

"What about the Jarawara people?" K.J. asked. "Have they moved much?"

Miguel scratched his head. "No. But remember there are six Jarawara villages. This one hasn't moved in fifteen years—because of Dr. Jones. He prays faithfully for these people. It makes a difference."

Everyone smiled, but Jeff couldn't get his mind off She'a. He didn't feel right leaving the boy alone with the shaman. Yet all the Indian men had gone back to work.

Jeff looked at Mindy and K.J. "We've got to do something. Let's see if we can tell what the shaman is doing."

K.J. liked the idea, but Mindy became frightened. "Should we be messing with their spiritual leader?"

"I just want to get closer. Then we'll pray."

Jeff led the team to a tree behind the shaman's house. Shivers suddenly ran up his back. "Did you hear that?"

K.J. nodded. "That's the wildest noise I've ever heard. Sounds like he's possessed with the devil all right."

Mindy grabbed Jeff's arm. "It's some kind of weird chanting."

"Let's pray and stand against it," Jeff said. "I think all this is happening because we prayed against the curse over this place. I'll keep my eyes open to see what's going on."

Everyone agreed and began praying. Jeff, who was facing the shaman's house, saw that the Jarawara men were hard at work again. Even though they looked over once in a while, they probably thought that he, K.J., and Mindy were still resting.

Then he heard a noise. He was surprised to see the shaman, carrying She'a, appear on the doorstep. The boy looked sicker than ever. Sweat poured from the ten-year-old's forehead.

Jeff and the others ducked behind the tree, but the shaman stopped right beside them. He stared coldly at Jeff. Jeff felt shivers again. Scowling, the shaman hurried toward the nearby stream.

"We're in trouble now," Jeff said. "I hope we're not going to cause Dr. Jones any problems."

"Yeah," K.J. agreed. "But did you see the shaman's eyes?"

Mindy was shaking. "Man, he sure looked possessed."

Jeff, Mindy, and K.J. decided to follow at a distance. The shaman splashed water on the boy's face as he continued his evil chant.

"At least," Mindy whispered, "the cool water will help bring the fever down."

Jeff looked at the others. "We'd better get back to work."

Everyone nodded and left the shaman and She'a to join the others.

❖ ❖ ❖ ❖ ❖ ❖ ❖

By afternoon, the clinic was nearing completion. Jeff was still wondering what had happened to She'a when Miguel appeared. He looked concerned.

"I need to talk to you," Miguel said. "We've got a little more trouble than we bargained for."

"What now?" Jeff asked.

"One of Dr. Jones's best friends, a Jarawara man, just told me something you need to know."

"What? What?" Mindy cried.

"The shaman is spreading the word that he just had a vision from the spirits."

"What was it?" Jeff grew worried.

"He's telling them there will be more fires and more sickness if they fight the landowners. He's saying that you guys are bringing some of it on."

Jeff dropped his head. "Oh great."

"There's more. He thinks She'a's illness is proof that he's right. And that if Chief Naati continues to fight, there will be much more illness."

"What are the people saying?" Mindy asked.

"They want to hear from Chief Naati and Dr. Jones."

K.J. got angry. "He's trying to destroy their morale! But they're still working on the clinic."

Jeff smiled at Miguel, realizing how hard it must have been for him to tell them the news. "Thanks for telling us."

Jeff knew the shaman was angry with them for trying to interfere, and he knew they had to pray. He looked at his watch. It was five in the afternoon.

Suddenly, all the Jarawara men dropped their tools and ran into the forest. Jeff was puzzled until he heard the faint roar of an engine in the distance. It had to be Warren, Dr. Jones, and Chief Naati returning.

Jeff knew the people were anxious to hear from the chief and Dr. Jones. The team followed the crowd. Jeff glanced to see where the shaman was, but he wasn't there.

The Cessna 206 rolled to a stop on the dirt runway. Jeff couldn't wait to hear the news. And maybe Dr. Jones could deal with the shaman.

The Indians cheered when the door opened. Chief Naati climbed out first, followed by Warren and Dr. Jones. The pilot handed Warren a familiar-looking bag and waved as he closed the door.

Jeff knew the bag contained K.J.'s equipment, but at the moment, it didn't seem important. Everyone stepped back while the plane turned around and took off, but all eyes were on the passengers.

Chief Naati was greeted by the village leaders. By now, Jeff thought he must be hearing about his son's illness and the shaman's vision.

Jeff and the team joined Warren. "What happened?" Jeff asked. "Good news?"

Warren smiled, handing the bag to K.J. "Here, K.J., carry this. I'd say getting our equipment back was good news. Dr. Jones is a powerful man."

K.J. hugged his camera bag. "What about the court decision?"

"That doesn't look so good."

Chapter 11

Miracle

What do you mean, Warren?" Jeff asked.

Just then, Dr. Jones joined them. The crowd started back to the village.

"I'll let Dr. Jones explain." Warren shrugged, looking exhausted. "Let's wait till we get back to his house."

"I don't know if I can wait," Jeff said.

Warren smiled. "Relax. We'll tell you everything."

Everyone hurried to the village, especially when they got close enough to smell dinner cooking. Jeff wanted to hear about the day in court, but he was hungry too.

Warren gasped when he spotted the clinic. "I don't believe it! It's almost finished!"

With astonished smiles, Dr. Jones and Warren surveyed the work. Dr. Jones spent a while hugging everyone in sight to thank them for all their hard work.

"How could they do this in one day?" Warren wanted to know.

Dr. Jones shook his head. "In all my years here, I've never seen anything go up so fast. At this rate, we can have the clinic open by Friday. Tomorrow, we'll organize the inside. There isn't much to put away."

"Can we help?" Mindy was eager to do all she could.

"Not tomorrow," Dr. Jones replied. "I heard you worked very hard today. Besides, Chief Naati really wants to show you the way the Jarawara live. The men have been planning to take you fishing. Miguel will go along to translate." A grin crossed his face from one side to the other. "He probably didn't tell you, but Miguel only comes here for the fishing."

K.J. got excited, but Mindy wasn't sure. "Are there hikes like the one we had the other day? And alligators?"

Everyone laughed but Mindy. Gently, Dr. Jones put his arm around her shoulders. "Young lady, you'll be very safe—the Jarawara know how to handle every danger around here."

"Are there wild animals out there?" Mindy cried.

"I hope so." Dr. Jones laughed. "You'll want to see some of them. Especially since you have your video equipment back."

"Yeah," K.J. said excitedly. "I'd do anything to get some footage of a jaguar. Or an alligator. Up close."

"Stay away from me," Mindy snapped. "I'll stick to fishing."

Everyone laughed and went inside for dinner. Miguel offered them fruit juice as they sat down. Jeff couldn't wait another second to hear about what had happened to Dr. Jones and Chief Naati, but he tried to be patient.

"Getting your equipment back was a real victory," Dr. Jones finally began. "It seems Mr. Giles influenced the government officials to take your equipment away. He told them you were going to use it to shut down all logging—and the Amazonian economy with it."

Jeff's mouth fell open. "I don't believe him! He really is evil."

Dr. Jones agreed. "The landowners don't want films about Indians going to the outside world—especially stories on how the villagers are being mistreated. The exposure such a film could bring is the landowners' worst nightmare."

"I can see that," Jeff said.

"I've built lots of friendships with government officials since I've been here. The head of the Indian Foundation is a friend of mine. I told them the truth about who you were. They said they were very sorry."

Jeff couldn't wait any longer. "What happened in court?"

Dr. Jones nodded to Warren to tell the rest of the story.

"When we arrived," Warren said, "the judge had made up his mind to keep things the way they were. He's had lots of pressure from landowners. Maybe even payoffs in the past."

"So what happened?" Mindy asked.

"Dr. Jones told the judge about the fire and listed some past human rights violations. When the judge heard this, he decided to hold off his decision until Monday."

"Why would he do that?" K.J. put down the juice he was drinking.

"He ordered an investigation. If he finds out Mr. Giles had anything to do with the fire, he may change his mind. Maybe the fire was the turning point."

"I told you guys that!" Jeff said, slapping K.J. on the arm. "What was Mr. Giles doing?"

Both Warren and Dr. Jones chuckled.

"Mr. Giles tried to hide his feelings," Dr. Jones said, "but he was squirming a bit in his seat."

"Let's pray the truth comes out," Warren added.

Everyone agreed. Jeff looked at Dr. Jones. "We need to tell you something about She'a. He got sick today. The shaman took him to his house and did weird things."

Dr. Jones nodded.

"I think the shaman is mad because we followed him," Jeff continued. "He's telling everybody he had a vision. He said that if the tribe fights the landowners anymore, there will be more sickness."

Dr. Jones smiled. "That doesn't surprise me. He has a lot of strange visions and dreams."

"He does?" Jeff asked, astonished.

"Jeff, anyone working with Indian tribes has to deal with shamans. What you saw is pretty normal."

"But nothing happened when he tried to heal She'a," Jeff pointed out. "In fact, She'a is much worse. He could be dying right now. The shaman doesn't know Jesus has the true power to heal!"

"I've been able to pray for the Jarawara many times," Dr. Jones said. "And I've seen people healed. But out of respect for their customs, I have to wait until they ask. Hard as it is for me sometimes, I have to respect their spiritual leader."

"I hope we didn't blow it," Jeff said.

"What does the shaman think when people are healed because of your prayers?" Mindy broke in.

"He knows I have access to some kind of healing power, but he still thinks his is greater. I'm not surprised She'a is sick. There's a spiritual attack going on—a battle for the Jarawaras' very survival."

"Well." Jeff smiled. "We know the devil is the source of the shaman's vision."

They all grew quiet. Moments later, Chief Naati called Dr. Jones outside. Dr. Jones stood, stretched, and plodded out of the building. He looked exhausted after his long day.

The team waited inside. Dinner was smelling better and better all the time.

Suddenly, Dr. Jones rushed back in. "Chief Naati says She'a is very sick. He's afraid his son is dying. He's asked us to come and pray."

Jeff and Mindy slapped their hands together. K.J. grabbed his camera.

Warren leaned over to K.J. "You'll need to be sensitive with that thing. Chief Naati has okayed the filming, but he many not want you to film anything this personal."

Quickly, everyone bowed their heads to commit the next few minutes to the Lord. Then they respectfully followed Chief Naati to his home.

Inside the chief's home, Jeff saw the history of the Jarawara tribe before his eyes. It looked like a museum. A huge jaguar pelt hung on the main wall. The eyes seemed to be looking right at him. An assortment of spears, bows, and arrows were arranged in a corner. Drawings of hunters, fishermen, and canoes decorated the walls.

Jeff followed Chief Naati to a back room where She'a was lying, deathly ill, on his hammock. To Jeff's shock, the shaman stood beside She'a, shaking a gourd over his body. Jeff assumed Chief Naati wanted the shaman there since he was the spiritual leader. The boy's mother stood off to one side.

Dr. Jones moved closer. He slipped a thermometer under She'a's tongue. Everyone waited in silence.

Moments later, Dr. Jones lifted the thermometer to the light. "One hundred and five degrees. He is very sick."

Jeff looked at She'a's feverish body. In spite of all the tricks the shaman had tried, the chief's son seemed to be getting worse instead of better.

Jeff went over and touched She'a's arm. Mindy, K.J., and Warren looked on. The shaman shook the gourd viciously within inches of Jeff's head. Dr. Jones continued to examine She'a.

"Years ago, I was miraculously healed," Jeff whispered to the doctor. "Do you think I could tell Chief Naati about it?"

First the doctor, then Chief Naati nodded.

"When I was young, I was in a serious car accident," Jeff began, waiting for the doctor to translate. "The doctors said I wouldn't live. In the hospital, I had a dream of Jesus coming into my room. I felt Him touch me. I was instantly healed. Then I asked Jesus to be my Lord and Savior."

K.J. had his camcorder focused and was filming everything. Chief Naati didn't seem to mind.

"Jesus said if we pray in His name," Jeff went on, "we can be healed. Chief Naati, you have asked us to pray for She'a. We believe Jesus will make his fever go away."

Dr. Jones finished the translation. The chief nodded. His eyes were moist.

Jeff motioned for everyone to join him. Since the beginning of the Reel Kids Club, Warren had always encouraged Jeff to take the lead. Everyone gathered around the boy. The shaman watched from a distance.

Jeff bowed his head. "Lord Jesus, we come in Your powerful name. Please show She'a and his father Your power."

Suddenly, She'a's eyes fluttered and looked around. No one was more shocked than Jeff. He'd seen people healed before, but never this fast.

Jeff looked up. Dr. Jones moved closer to the boy. He stuck the thermometer back under his tongue.

Everyone waited in silent astonishment. She'a's eyes alternately opened and closed. He looked confused about why people were gathered in his bedroom.

Dr. Jones pulled out the thermometer and held it to the light of the kerosene lamp. "His temperature is normal. This is a miracle! He's been healed."

Chapter 12

Fishing Trip

Everyone was speechless. The shaman stomped out the door. Chief Naati fell on his son, weeping. She'a's mother rushed in to hug both her husband and her boy at the same time.

After a moment, the chief looked up at Jeff and grasped his hand. Then he mumbled a few words to Dr. Jones.

With a growing smile, Dr. Jones translated. "He wants to thank you, Jeff. He knows now how powerful your God is."

Jeff was awed at God's power. He felt humbled. He wanted to find a place to hide and cry for a while. "Tell him we had nothing to do with this. It was God."

At dinner, the chief told his people what had happened to his son. A celebration followed, and the whole village rejoiced—except the angry shaman. He sat away from the group. K.J. got some great shots with his wide angle lens.

❖ ❖ ❖ ❖ ❖ ❖ ❖

Thursday morning came much too fast for Jeff. He was still tired from all that had happened the day before. Then he heard Miguel's smooth Brazilian voice.

"Time to get up," Miguel announced.

Jeff rolled over in his hammock to see his smiling friend. "What time is it?" he moaned.

Miguel chuckled. "It almost five, you sleepy heads. Fishing starts early around here."

Miguel left. Jeff tossed a pillow at K.J. "Get up. Time to fish."

Warren raised his head and readjusted his pillow. "Have fun fishing. I'm going to stay here and help set up the clinic—after I sleep another minute or two."

Jeff grunted. Trying to untangle himself from the swinging hammock, he fell to the floor with a thud. K.J. and Warren laughed.

Jeff and K.J. ate fruit and bread for breakfast. Mindy was outside waiting for them.

"You guys are a little late, aren't you?" she teased.

"Lay off," K.J. said. "We need more beauty sleep than you."

Jeff spotted Dr. Jones setting up makeshift tables at the clinic. He hurried over.

"Your visit to the Amazon was perfectly timed." Dr. Jones smiled. "God is up to something big, and you're part of it."

Jeff tried to hide his embarrassment. "We're honored to be here, sir."

With his arm around his son, Chief Naati joined them. Amazingly, the boy looked as strong as ever.

"She'a wants to take you and the others fishing," Dr. Jones translated for Chief Naati. "After yesterday, he's especially happy to be alive."

Chief Naati motioned for Jeff and the others to watch Miguel and the Jarawara men prepare to go fishing. The men were furiously pounding green plants with wooden sticks.

"What are they doing?" Jeff asked Miguel.

"They've got a special way of fishing. It's popular among many of the Indian tribes in Latin America."

"What does beating plants have to do with fishing?" K.J. asked as he positioned his camera.

Miguel laughed. "Believe it or not, it does. They're pounding a root to get poison out of it. Inside is a milky liquid that poisons the fish."

"Poisoned fish? And it doesn't poison people?" Mindy asked.

Miguel laughed again. "No. It's the same fish you've been eating all week. The poison doesn't affect the meat, but it stuns the fish for a few seconds and it paralyzes their breathing system."

"Isn't that a little unfair?" Mindy was doubtful.

"When the fish are stunned, the men line up with bows and arrows to shoot them."

Mindy shook her head. "I guess that sounds a lit-tle more fair. Why don't they use nets?"

Miguel laughed, shaking his head. "They do that too. They fish all kinds of ways. You'll see."

After the men collected the milky substance in handmade wooden containers, they were ready to go. Besides Miguel and She'a, about six other men and a few women were going along.

As they headed down the trail, Jeff realized how much he liked the exotic sights and sounds. He stud-ied the lush, dense, tropical vegetation along the way. They hiked through the garden clearings that were scattered throughout the jungle. Ragged roots and mud holes made them pay attention to what was ahead.

They made a game of pushing back long vines that hung from the towering trees. K.J. kept his cam-era rolling so he wouldn't miss a thing.

Once away from the village, Jeff listened to the hush of the jungle. At first, all he heard were foot-steps hitting the dirt path. This was different from any world he had ever known. Green backdrops were accented by brilliant birds, exotic flowers, and changing skies. It was as if God poured out His best creative efforts here.

As he listened more closely, Jeff heard more. To accompany the lush foliage, God had created new sounds, orchestrated by nature itself. Crickets, frogs, clicking butterflies, rustling leaves, and the songs of a dozen birds made the jungle rich and alive. It was a part of God's creation Jeff had never known. He felt as if he were strolling through a huge cathedral. He was filled with awe.

Suddenly, the beauty was interrupted. Jeff's heart almost stopped as he looked through some trees to an open area. With his eyes nearly bulging out of his head, he turned to Miguel. "What is it?"

"A deer, I think. But it's twisted or caught or something. Could that be a snake?"

Everyone behind them stopped. Two Jarawara men rushed toward the animal.

"It's a boa constrictor!" Miguel cried out.

Jeff had seen boas at the zoo, but never this close and never loose in the wild. Approaching slowly behind the men, Jeff saw the huge snake. At first, it looked like a green and brown vine twisted at a strange angle.

Looking closer, Jeff saw a flat, triangular head with a forked tongue darting in and out. The snake must have been at least fourteen feet long. Inside its deadly crush was a small deer who had obviously been caught unaware. K.J. moved in with his camera.

Miguel turned to Jeff. "The snake has killed the deer, but not eaten it yet. Too bad you can't watch that—it's an incredible sight. But the Jarawara will kill the snake and take the deer."

Sure enough, the men lifted their machetes. They hacked away at the huge reptile as fast as they could.

"Look," Mindy said with a sigh of relief, "the deer is already dead. The poor thing didn't have a chance."

The men pulled the deer from the snake's grip.

"Is it okay to eat?" Jeff asked.

"Yes," Miguel said. "It's probably only been dead for a few minutes. But the Jarawara won't eat anything that's been strangled."

"Why's that?" Jeff asked.

"Superstition." Miguel smiled.

"What will they do with the deer, then?" Mindy asked.

"They'll clean it up and take it with us, then sell it to the river traders."

"Think they'd sell me a piece?" K.J. asked with a snicker. "I'd love some deer meat for dinner."

Everyone laughed as they continued down the trail. About an hour later, they arrived at a narrow stream, and the men prepared to fish. Miguel explained this was the tribe's favorite place to fish. Here they caught a brightly colored fish called peacock bass.

"Watch closely," Miguel said. "This is one of the best things you'll learn on how a tribe gets their food. The Indians make a real social event out of it. Even the women and children go. They usually make a full day of it."

Jeff quietly picked up K.J.'s camera. She'a was showing K.J. and Mindy how to use his bow and arrow. They laughed and laughed as arrows flew every way but at the target.

Jeff knew fishing was a big part of life for the Jarawara, so he had brought a package of fish hooks from home. With a bit of ceremony, he presented one to She'a. Grinning, She'a promptly stuck it in his pierced ear. The others looked on appreciatively, and Jeff passed out the rest of the package. Soon almost every Jarawara man sported a fish hook in his ear. She'a had started a fashion trend.

The men took out the milky substance. Pouring it out of the containers, they lined the stream with it, then waited with bows and arrows. Even Mindy stood poised and ready to shoot. K.J. reclaimed the camera from Jeff, took a new videotape out and began filming.

Jeff watched with amazement. In less than two minutes, fish popped to the surface.

"Look at them!" K.J. said.

Jeff couldn't believe it. One, two, three—arrows began to fly.

"This is amazing!" K.J. said with a chuckle. "Those fish are sitting ducks."

Two Jarawara men ran knee deep into the water with a basket in one hand and a machete in the other. With one swift motion, they cut off the fish's heads, then tossed the limp fish into the basket.

Watching Mindy, Jeff doubled over with laughter. Every time she lifted the bow, the arrow fell off. K.J. was laughing so hard he couldn't hold the camera still. The Jarawara were much more polite.

"Why don't you try it, K.J.?" Mindy challenged.

"Sure," K.J. responded. "But Jeff needs to run the camcorder. I don't want to miss a thing."

K.J. got a bow and some arrows from She'a. Climbing up on a log, he moved as close to the water's edge as possible. Jeff started the camcorder again.

K.J. shot his first arrow. It sunk into the water.

Mindy snickered. "See, K.J. Not that easy, is it?"

K.J. grinned. "Well, at least I got it off the bow."

Through the camera lens, Jeff suddenly noticed movement in the jungle behind K.J. He quickly tapped Miguel on the shoulder and pointed to the bushes. "What is it?"

Miguel's face grew pale. "A jaguar."

Chapter 13

Every Tribe

Some of the Jarawara men were watching the big cat. K.J. looked up, excited. Mindy was still concentrating on fishing and hadn't noticed the jaguar.

In a rush, K.J. tossed the bow to She'a and reached for the camcorder. He tiptoed toward the jaguar. Suddenly, he stopped, looking back. "What if he comes after me?"

Miguel followed him. The cat stood still, watching every move. "Don't worry. I don't think he'll attack. There are too many people around."

She'a saw the jaguar and ran to K.J.'s side. When Mindy noticed, her eyes grew big as saucers. Slowly, she moved closer to Jeff.

111

Miguel whispered to K.J. "Be quiet or it'll run away."

Jeff joined them, watching as the cat intently watched them. "He is a beautiful animal."

Everyone moved cautiously. The Jarawara men were used to seeing such animals in the jungle. They were cautious and aware, but not frightened.

Silently, K.J. moved closer, and the others followed. Suddenly, the jaguar decided K.J. had gotten close enough. He bared his teeth and hissed threateningly. K.J. held the camera still and filmed.

Jeff and Mindy froze. The jaguar went down on his belly, ready to attack. Suddenly the jungle was filled with the cat's ear-shattering roar. K.J. stood motionless, his finger still on the red button of the camcorder.

Closer and closer the large cat moved. Jeff could see long, sharp teeth. With Mindy clinging to his arm, Jeff watched in wonder. Suddenly She'a ran between K.J. and the jaguar. Then the ten-year-old opened his mouth and made a wild, frightening noise.

Immediately, the jaguar stopped in its tracks. He stared at She'a for a moment, and everyone watched in awe. Then the jaguar roared one last time and walked away.

K.J. collapsed on a nearby tree stump. "Boy. For a moment I thought I was dead meat."

Jeff sighed with relief. "Me too."

Miguel smiled, putting his arm around She'a.

K.J. looked at She'a and Miguel. "Tell him thanks for saving my life."

Miguel translated, then he grinned at K.J. "He

says you saved his life with your prayers. He's glad to save yours."

Everyone laughed.

❖❖❖❖❖❖❖

Hours later, the fish were collected. Even Jeff and K.J. had caught two each.

"We're ready to head back," Miguel said.

"I'm ready." Mindy nodded. "I don't know if I can handle much more of the jungle."

As the men hoisted the baskets of fish onto their shoulders, Jeff and the others took one last look around. K.J. was still filming everything. Jeff looked into a clearing. To his surprise, three men were headed straight for them. As they approached, Jeff was stunned to recognize them.

It was Mr. Giles! And he was carrying a rifle. Manuel, the strange man on the canoe, was beside him. The third man was a very large Brazilian with an angry look on his face. He, too, carried a gun.

Miguel ran to Jeff's side. When the Jarawaras backed away at the appearance of Mr. Giles and his men, Jeff saw the power the landowners had over the Indians.

He turned to Miguel. "What'll we do?"

"Nothing. Let's just see what they want."

Mr. Giles strutted over to Jeff and Miguel. The Jarawaras retreated into the brush.

With an evil sneer on his face, Mr. Giles stopped. "Who gave you permission to hunt here?"

Jeff didn't say anything. He was too frightened.

Mr. Giles stepped closer. "This is my land. Who gave you permission to hunt here?"

Jeff couldn't hold back anymore. He shook off the fear he felt. "This isn't your land. It belongs to the Jarawara, and you know it."

Mindy raced up. Jeff glanced over his shoulder to see where K.J. was. He saw only the unmistakable lens of the camcorder sticking out from behind a tree. It was pointed straight at Mr. Giles.

Mr. Giles looked at Jeff, laughing loudly. "What do you American kids know about my land? I warned you not to come here."

Jeff squared his shoulders and looked him in the eye. "We know the truth, Mr. Giles. And it won't be long before the court reveals it to you."

Mr. Giles' face reddened. "If you're smart, you'll get on the first plane out of here. Or maybe you'll have to experience another accident in the village."

Jeff became angry. "So you started that fire!"

"So what?" Mr. Giles scorned. "They're only Indians. Next time it'll be the whole village." He looked at Mindy. "You're only making things worse for them. And don't tell me you're not interested in making money off these savages."

Jeff couldn't believe his ears.

Then Mr. Giles walked over to She'a and looked him up and down. He laughed. "So this is the Chief's son?"

She'a had been half-hidden behind Jeff. Now he backed off slowly. Jeff knew he was frightened.

Simultaneously, Jeff and Miguel stepped between She'a and Mr. Giles. "Leave him alone," Jeff demanded.

Mr. Giles laughed louder still. Then an older Jarawara man walked up and joined Jeff and Miguel. Jeff was proud of him.

Mr. Giles looked at the Indian. Then he turned to Manuel and the other man, who had been laughing among themselves. The Brazilian held his gun pointed at them.

Mr. Giles gave a quick order to Manuel. Manuel slid a knife out of his belt and moved around Jeff and Miguel to get to She'a. Everyone froze. Jeff felt helpless.

Manuel put the knife against She'a's throat and looked him in the eye.

Jeff raised his hand in protest.

With a slow chuckle, Mr. Giles ordered Manuel to stop.

"Tell Dr. Jones if he doesn't back off, this boy may lose his life."

Jeff didn't move. Mr. Giles eyes looked hard and cold. He shook his head and turned to walk away.

Just as Mr. Giles turned, Jeff heard a branch crack where K.J. was hiding. Unfortunately, Manuel heard it too. He turned to the spot and saw K.J. behind the tree. Manuel raced over. He jerked K.J. by the arm and pulled him out.

K.J. shook off his grasp and stepped back. In a surprise move, She'a ran over and yanked K.J. away from Manuel. Then as quick as a wink, they both disappeared into the dense jungle.

Mr. Giles lifted his gun and aimed in that direction.

Without thinking, Jeff reached out, whacking the barrel of the rifle. Mr. Giles was knocked off balance. A shot was fired. Mr. Giles pushed Jeff to the ground and pointed the rifle at him. He looked so angry that Jeff was afraid he'd shoot.

"Your friend better give us that tape," Mr. Giles whispered through clenched teeth, "or we'll kill one of you."

Jeff looked toward where K.J. and She'a had run. It was as if the jungle had swallowed them whole.

Then Mr. Giles and his men ran after them.

Jeff turned to Miguel. "If he finds them, will he kill them?"

"He'll never find them," Miguel replied. "She'a knows every inch of this jungle. He'll hide until they leave. Don't worry. Let's head back. The Jarawara will find us on the trail."

❖❖❖❖❖❖

Jeff and the others had been on the trail nearly an hour when She'a and K.J. suddenly popped out of a bush.

"About time you guys get here," K.J. said with his most charming grin. "She'a is good."

She'a was smiling.

Jeff hugged both of them. "Boy, are we glad to see you! Let's get back to the village before they find your trail."

K.J. grinned. "Yeah. And we'd better hide this tape. Mr. Giles is going to want it real bad now. I viewed it while we were waiting for you. Everything he said came out loud and clear."

Soon, to his relief, Jeff saw the village. He couldn't wait to tell Warren and Dr. Jones what happened. He almost forgot about the fish and the deer the men were carrying.

Breathing hard, Jeff explained everything to Warren, Dr. Jones, and Chief Naati.

"What a story!" Warren exclaimed. "Where should we hide the tape?"

Dr. Jones whispered something to Chief Naati. Then the Chief spoke back.

"Chief Naati says the best place to hide it is in his house. No one will enter his home."

"Sounds good to us," Jeff said.

K.J. handed the tape to the chief. Jeff hoped it would be safe.

After dinner, the team talked to Dr. Jones at his new house. The men had been busy making furniture all day, and it was already filling up.

"We've got to be on our toes," Warren warned. "It seems Mr. Giles will do anything to get his way. Even kill."

Mindy looked up. "What if he comes to the village with that gun?"

Dr. Jones became serious. "We'll have to face that when it happens."

Warren tried to smile. "Let's forget it for now. I've asked Dr. Jones to share with you why tribes are so important to God."

Jeff was excited. He was fascinated by Dr. Jones's work and wanted to learn all he could. And he wanted to get Mr. Giles off his mind.

As Dr. Jones began, his eyes teared up. "I love these people. They're a beautiful expression of God's creativity and diversity. Sadly, not everyone likes people who are different from themselves."

K.J. looked up. "We know one guy like that."

Dr. Jones nodded. "Yes. And sad to say, it causes wars."

"Boy," Jeff said, "that happens in Los Angeles all the time. We have Whites, African Americans, Asians, Hispanics, and a host of other groups. They're always fighting with each other. Think what could happen if we could all see the good in our differences."

"Right," Dr. Jones agreed. "God made us all different. Just think how many varieties of birds and fish God made. He wanted us to enjoy them all."

Mindy laughed. "K.J.'s very different."

Everyone chuckled.

"Hey," K.J. said, taking a bow, "that's why you guys love me, right?"

"Sit down, K.J.," Warren said with a wry grin.

Dr. Jones went on. "People have oppressed tribes for years. They want to get rid of them. It causes the Indians to have a very low self-esteem."

"Can we change that?" Mindy asked.

"That's why I came," Dr. Jones said. "I want to give the Jarawara an understanding of their true identity."

"How?" Jeff asked.

"By helping the tribe to read and write in their own language. Then they will see the beauty of their culture and pass it on to their kids. This keeps tribes alive for generations."

"I don't understand," Mindy said.

Dr. Jones smiled. "I'll explain. Language and Bible translation are the most important works I know. Even though I'm a doctor, I realize language learning gives the tribe a future. That's why I focus strongly on it."

"What's a bummer," Jeff said, "is that all your books went up in smoke."

"It isn't as bad as it seems. Luckily, I have copies of all my work in Labrea. Something told me to have that done only a month or so ago."

"That's great news." Jeff was relieved. "Tell us more about your language studies."

"When people write out their stories, they see their own history and identity. Then they pass it on to their kids and so on."

Mindy's eyes lit up. "It makes them feel good about themselves—like they matter in the world."

"That's right," Dr. Jones said. "And when they feel good about themselves, they'll improve their village and build dignity into their children."

"What have you written out?" Warren wanted to know.

"Language, health guidelines, farm manuals, and the Bible. My wife was teaching the people to read, but I haven't been able to work with them much since she died. We prepared books for the children to learn—primers, writing guides, and math and social studies. Education is so important. More and more, these children will be exposed to the world."

"Wow," K.J. said. "I used to laugh at missionaries who did translation work. I thought that was for old ladies who wore their hair pinned up in buns."

Dr. Jones smiled. "Landowners don't like us teaching the Indians because then they can't be controlled. But without education, tribes are killed or driven from their homes. Then the people dwindle away. It's happened to thousands of tribes that Jesus loves."

Mindy shook her fist. "It's not going to happen to the Jarawara!"

"My wife and I spent years building dignity and worth. I'd love to help them accept Jesus."

"Do you think the Jarawara are close to making that decision?" Jeff asked.

"I think so," Dr. Jones said.

Chapter 14

Turning Point

Jeff crawled out of bed early Friday morning. He was thankful for what he'd learned from Dr. Jones. He thought about God's desire to redeem every culture.

He was also excited. Today they could finally film Dr. Jones ministering to the Jarawaras and Brazilians with his medical skills. It would be terrific footage.

After a breakfast of papaya, grapefruit, and bread, K.J. tinkered with the camcorder. Mindy helped Dr. Jones with final preparations.

On his way to the clinic, Jeff noticed a few village women hurrying in one direction. Then the men ran over. Jeff was curious, so he went too.

His newsman instincts kicked in as he approached the group of people, and he hollered for K.J. to bring the camera. Where there was a crowd, there was usually a story and a photo opportunity. Mindy came running.

"This place is just full of surprises!" Jeff yelled to his sister.

On the jungle side of a house, Jeff saw the most unusual sight. At first it looked like a long shadow on the ground, but the sun was shining directly on it. Jeff guessed it was two feet wide.

"Look," K.J. said, peering into the lens. "It's moving."

Jeff looked down. Slowly and steadily, the shadow was moving. Jeff realized this was the area where the men had cleaned the fish the day before.

The ground seemed to be in motion, heaving and swaying. The mysterious shape zigzagged this way and that, like an optical illusion. He shook his head. When he focused on the edge of the shape, he saw what it was.

"Ants!" Jeff exclaimed. "Millions of 'em!"

"I don't believe it," Mindy cried. "I've never seen anything like that in my life."

"You haven't lived that long," K.J. laughed, filming.

The main column was just a few feet away.

"They're huge! They must be three-quarters of an inch long," Jeff said. "They're packed in there so tightly, they must be holding hands!"

The team heard chuckling behind them. When they turned around, a roar of laughter went up. The entire tribe was laughing so hard that they were holding their sides. K.J., Jeff, and Mindy realized the tribe was being entertained by the their response. They joined in the laughter.

After a minute, the party atmosphere died down, and most of the tribe went back to work. Jeff looked at Miguel. "Can they be stopped? They're still pouring out of the jungle."

"Watch and see." Miguel smiled.

Jeff squatted to watch closely. Mindy stepped back. Thousands of ants were already feasting on the leftover fragments of fish. A Jarawara man appeared with a five-gallon gas can and matches.

The crisscrossing ribbons of ants kept moving. Jeff's skin crawled. Carefully, the man poured gas in front of the procession, then lit the match.

Suddenly, there was a big poof followed by an orange flash. The muddy ground burned, but the main column kept coming. Then gas was poured on the sides and lit.

Jeff watched closely. The ants stopped. Slowly, and in perfect formation, they turned and marched back into the jungle.

Mindy let out a sigh of relief. "What if they decide to come back in them middle of the night. I think they could carry me away!"

"Boy, would I love to get that on film!" K.J. said.

Mindy gave him a dirty look.

"Just kidding, Mindy," K.J. said quickly. "Just kidding."

Dr. Jones called the team to his new home. As they entered, Jeff realized the photo of the woman with the dazzling smile was missing. It made him sad to think everything from Dr. Jones's home was gone.

But Dr. Jones didn't seem to be concentrating on the past. He was already moving on. After everyone was seated, Dr. Jones got serious. "We've got a problem. The shaman is pressuring Chief Naati to back off. Some leaders are starting to believe him and his dream."

"What can we do?" Mindy cried.

"This battle must be won in prayer," Dr. Jones said. "If the chief goes against the shaman, it could create a fight among the people."

"Let's spend some time in prayer," Jeff suggested.

The team cheered an amen.

After their prayer, everyone looked refreshed. Jeff felt that victory was close. "What if Chief Naati believes the shaman?" he asked.

"Fifteen years of my work will be lost," Dr. Jones replied sadly. "A chief can stand up against a shaman, but it'll take a miracle."

"God can do it," Mindy said quietly.

"What will it take to see a whole village come to Jesus?" K.J. asked.

"Time," Dr. Jones said. "Chief Naati must make the first decision in God's perfect timing."

"What do you mean?" K.J. pressed.

"If he decides to follow Jesus, the whole tribe will deny the shaman's ways and set up a new community. Eventually they will all accept Jesus and build a church among themselves."

"That would be so cool," Mindy said. "I've read books about such miracles, but it would be incredible to see it for myself."

Suddenly, someone was at the door, but it was too early for the clinic.

"It's Chief Naati," Mindy whispered in amazement.

"And She'a," Jeff said.

"God heard our prayers." K.J.'s eyes were big.

Dr. Jones invited Chief Naati and She'a to sit down. All eyes were fixed on the chief.

He looked at the club, then he turned to Dr. Jones. "I've been doing some serious thinking."

Dr. Jones asked if he wanted the words translated. Chief Naati nodded his head yes.

"I've watched you over the years," Chief Naati began. "You've taught us many things. But we still hold on to our views. We have always followed the shaman's spiritual guidance."

Chief Naati paused for a moment. Jeff was afraid what might be coming. The chief looked at his son. "You have shown us how special our tribe is. You have brought pride to our children."

She'a smiled.

"The shaman wants me to give up our land," Chief Naati continued. "He's had a warning in a dream."

The team listened carefully.

"I must decide."

Everyone scooted to the edge of their seats. Jeff gulped. "When She'a was healed," the chief went on, "something happened in my heart. I know now there is a much higher power than the shaman. I've made my decision."

Dr. Jones sat as still as a rock.

"And I make it for the whole tribe."

Everyone held their breath.

"I've spent the morning with the village leaders." Chief Naati looked at Dr. Jones. Tears came to his eyes. "I've decided. Our village will be a meeting place for Jesus."

Smiles dawned on every face. She'a beamed and nodded.

Jeff couldn't believe his ears. He didn't know what to do. He just sat there. Stunned. Quiet. Thrilled.

Dr. Jones looked up. Tears filled his eyes. He talked to Chief Naati. After a few minutes, he explained what they were talking about. "I asked him if the shaman knows of his decision."

"Does he?" Warren asked.

"The chief is giving him a chance to join too."

Suddenly, there was a sharp knock on the door. Dr. Jones opened it to a figure standing in the doorway.

It was the shaman.

Chapter 15

The Verdict

Everyone held their breath. Jeff looked at the tribe's spiritual guide, but he didn't seem angry. Chief Naati walked outside with him and Dr. Jones.

Everyone wondered what was going to happen next. Then Dr. Jones came back in, running his fingers through his greying hair. He plopped down.

"This is incredible," Dr. Jones said with tears rolling down his cheeks. "I've sowed seeds for fifteen years. We're about to see a harvest."

Mindy jumped up. "What did Chief Naati mean about making the village a meeting place for God?"

"He's changing the village value system.

127

Eventually everyone will become a follower of Jesus."

"Wow. Fifteen years!" Mindy said with admiration. "That's longer than I've been alive. You have taught me a huge lesson in patience."

"And it happened while we were here! How exciting it is to watch God work," Jeff said.

"I'm honored to have you here." Dr. Jones smiled. "It was perfect timing."

"We're the honored ones," K.J. put in. "I hope this film inspires thousands to work among tribal people."

"Yeah, I'm open," Mindy said. She paused. "Know of any tribes without ants or alligators?"

Everyone laughed.

"It's really a safe place," the doctor said.

"I guess we're just rookies," K.J. admitted with a laugh.

But Jeff couldn't get the shaman off his mind. What was he up to? "I wonder what's going on out there."

"That's not our problem," Dr. Jones said. "Chief Naati is a man of his word. He won't change his mind. Neither will his leaders."

"If only Mr. Giles would go home," Mindy cried.

"We'll leave that in God's hands," Dr. Jones said. He looked at his watch. "Time for the afternoon clinic! And time for the camera to roll."

As they were about to leave, Chief Naati came back in. Dr. Jones asked what had happened. Everybody waited while they spoke.

Finally, Dr. Jones filled them in. "The shaman is willing to change. He even wants to pronounce a blessing on the chief's house."

"What kind of blessing could a shaman pronounce?" Mindy asked warily.

"We'll see," Warren said.

Everyone smiled, but Jeff was still concerned.

❖❖❖❖❖❖❖

Monday morning came before they knew it. The weekend had been fun—filming, hiking, hunting, and getting to know the Jarawaras better. They had also learned much more from Dr. Jones.

Today was the day of the judge's decision. Dr. Jones had invited the club members to fly to Labrea with him and Warren. K.J. had video work to do, so he and Miguel decided to stay to get some final shots.

As Jeff and Mindy prepared to go, K.J. went to get the tape. Only a minute later, K.J. burst out of Chief Naati's house and came running.

"What's wrong?" Jeff asked.

K.J. was breathless, frantic. "Someone took the tape!"

The tribe went through the whole village, searching for over an hour. Jeff realized that finding the tape was hopeless. He almost certain Mr. Giles had it.

"We have to go," Dr. Jones said finally. "We'll have to go to court without the tape."

Chief Naati quickly spoke with Dr. Jones. The doctor nodded his head and turned to the team. "The chief has decided to stay here and keep the tribe together. He's still concerned about the shaman, who has also mysteriously disappeared."

Standing at the airstrip with Chief Naati and the tribe, Jeff was angry about the tape. He was also nervous about the judge's decision. It could change the tribe's destiny.

K.J. had his camcorder running. Jeff walked over to him. "Are you okay about staying here?"

K.J. smiled. "Remember, I got the plane ride yesterday. That was so cool. I got shots of the Perus River, canoes, alligators, everything. I'm fine. You go ahead."

"We were lucky the pilot had time," Jeff said.

K.J. nodded. "I'll be praying."

Jeff smiled. "Get that filming done. We leave tomorrow."

"I know. I know. And I'm not looking forward to the trip."

"Me either," Jeff groaned. "It's a long way from Porto Velho to L.A. I'm gonna sleep the whole way."

Dr. Jones and Warren motioned for Mindy and Jeff to get on board. Once inside, Jeff studied the cockpit. The instruments looked complex, even though it was a five-passenger Cessna. He couldn't wait to get in the air.

The engines roared, and they taxied down the runway. With a sudden burst of speed, the plane lifted off the ground. Jeff looked down as the plane circled toward Labrea. Below, he saw all the Jarawaras waving.

Mindy wiped away tears. Sitting next to the pilot, Dr. Jones wore the same grin he'd worn all weekend. Jeff knew his heart was full because of the chief's decision.

If only we had that tape, Jeff thought.

Flying over the jungle was an awesome sight. They had a much better view than they'd had in the cargo plane. And they were strapped in real seats this time.

When he spotted stacks of logs along the Perus River, Jeff understood the conflict over the trees. He thought about greed, and why men like Mr. Giles wanted everything.

A week ago, Jeff had never seen this place. Now the Jarawara village felt like home. Jeff loved the Amazon, the people, and everything about this country. He didn't feel like a stranger any more. And though Mr. Giles's parents had lived in the Amazon for years, the British man was the real stranger to the land. The Amazon stranger.

Jeff knew no matter how many times Mr. Giles visited, he would always be a stranger. Unless his heart changed.

Approaching Labrea, Jeff looked down at the community of 40,000 people. He thought of how the Peru Peru Indians had named the whole area "falling down sick." Jeff knew something had changed since they prayed for She'a. Now they needed to break the power of greed.

❖❖❖❖❖❖❖

The courtroom was before them. Jeff prayed silently. Out of the corner of his eye, he spotted Mr. Giles. Manuel and some other men were with him.

Mr. Giles walked right up. "You'll be leaving our country soon, I hope."

Mindy's face turned red. "Not before the court hearing."

Mr. Giles laughed. The other men snickered. Mr. Giles looked angrily at Mindy. "Shouldn't you be in school, little girl?"

Jeff knew his sister was getting angry. A Scripture popped into Jeff's mind: Let no one depise your youth. He knew it was found in Timothy. He thought how wrong Mr. Giles was about Mindy. Though she was only thirteen, God saw her as more than a little girl. Jesus had been only twelve when he astounded the teachers in the temple.

Mr. Giles wouldn't quit. "You guys almost had me on your film, didn't you? The shaman really blessed the chief's home, didn't he?"

Jeff was so angry he felt like slugging the man. He knew now how Mr. Giles had gotten the video. Jeff wondered how the shaman could betray his tribe.

Warren gathered the team away from Mr. Giles. Jeff and Mindy slowly followed him and Dr. Jones into the Labrea courtroom.

Inside, the white room was about the size of a classroom. The engraved mahogany judge's bench was the focus in the front. Jeff noticed the President's picture hanging behind the bench. The Brazilian flag stood next to the Amazon flag, covered with white stars. Jeff looked at his watch. The hearing was to begin at eleven. They had ten minutes. Quietly, they took their seats.

"This is one of the most important moments in Jarawara history," Warren said. "And for other tribes too."

"I know," Jeff said. "I'm really nervous."

Warren patted Jeff's arm. "Indians have lost other cases around the nation of Brazil."

"But we've got to win this one," Jeff whispered. He looked over at Mindy. She was twisting a strand of hair, which told him she was still angry.

Moments passed.

Mr. Giles walked in, flanked by his men. They took their seats opposite Dr. Jones and the team.

A door opened, and the judge walked in. He was a fiftyish, dignified-looking man wearing a black robe. Everyone rose when he approached his bench.

The judge leafed through a file of papers.

Jeff bit his fingernails. Mindy still played with her hair. The judge turned toward the man in charge of investigating the matter. "Have you found any violation of human rights by Mr. Giles?"

The investigator stood. "Sir, I have talked to many Brazilians who work in the Jarawara area. My investigation has shown no proof that Mr. Giles has done anything wrong."

Mindy turned beet red. Jeff knew she wanted to stand up and protest. So did he.

"Mindy," he whispered, "be still and know that He is God."

Mindy looked at Jeff. "I'm angry. They're all on his side! He probably paid them off."

The investigator went on. "I'm very concerned about Dr. Jones and his visitors from America. Mr. Giles has showed me some footage of a video they're making. It shows the Indians misusing the land."

Jeff was ready to explode. Mr. Giles had obviously shown him only one part of the video footage and created some phony story to go along with it. Jeff felt helpless.

The judge thanked the investigator and turned

to Dr. Jones. "Dr. Jones, do you have anything to say for the Jarawaras?"

Calmly, Dr. Jones stood to his feet. "Sir, I've worked with the Jarawara people for fifteen years. Over and over, I've seen them cheated out of fair wages. They've been taken advantage of and had their rights violated countless times."

Dr. Jones looked down at a piece of paper. "I have records that go way back. Mr. Giles has not stayed on his own property but continually trespasses on Indian land. That video you saw was phony. The Indians deserve their ancestral land." He sat down.

The judge asked Mr. Giles to speak. Standing up, he smirked at the club. Then he faced the judge. "Sir, whenever I visit my property, I've made sure my men treat the Jarawara people with respect."

Jeff couldn't believe his ears! Mr. Giles was lying through his teeth.

"My family has treated the Indians well for years," Mr. Giles said smoothly. "I don't know what the problem is. I propose that the land remain as it is."

Mindy looked close to an explosion. Mr. Giles was greedy and evil.

The judge thanked Mr. Giles, then he addressed the court. "Based on the information I have now, I'm going to make a ruling. My decision is in favor of Mr. Giles."

Chapter 16

New Identity

Jeff was shocked. Mindy was livid. Warren turned to Dr. Jones. "What are we going to tell Chief Naati?"

"I don't know," Dr. Jones said sadly. "I honestly didn't expect this."

Jeff and the others turned to leave. Mr. Giles snickered at them, then approached. "There's your justice. Now go home where you belong."

"The books will be balanced in the end," Mindy said through clenched teeth. "Then we'll all see real justice."

Jeff grabbed her arm and turned her away before

she could say any more. He knew he'd be sorry if he said anything. Discouragement filled his heart.

❖ ❖ ❖ ❖ ❖ ❖ ❖

Back at the village, Dr. Jones stayed inside his house. It had been hours since he had given the news to Chief Naati. The village was strangely quiet. Slowly, the team packed their gear for their trip home in the morning.

Jeff looked out at the Jarawara as they went about their business. He wondered how God could have failed them. I don't understand, Father, he silently prayed. Where were You?

"Well, I'm packed," Warren said. "I think I'm going to see how Dr. Jones is doing." He quietly left.

"It's not right," K.J. muttered after Warren walked out. "The Jarawara people don't deserve this."

Jeff didn't respond. He kept packing, his dark thoughts taunting him.

Suddenly, there was a commotion outside. The Jarawaras started running down the trail. Jeff knew this could only mean one thing—a plane was coming in. He looked at his watch. It was five o'clock. He knew there wasn't a plane scheduled to come in this evening.

K.J. grabbed his camera, and he and Jeff joined Mindy outside. Warren and Dr. Jones came out of the doctor's house looking confused.

Everyone raced to the airstrip.

The Cessna taxied to a stop. Everyone crowded around. Jeff saw the missionary pilot inside. His face was gleaming when he climbed out. "I've got good news!"

He handed Dr. Jones a note. Everyone waited as the doctor read.

"What is it? What is it?" Mindy finally cried.

Dr. Jones broke into a grin. "You won't believe it! A Brazilian man who worked for Mr. Giles told the judge everything—even how the video was stolen."

"What does that mean?" Jeff asked.

"The judge is reopening the case. He is recommending that I appeal his ruling. He is willing to give the land to the Indians. Criminal charges may be filed against Mr. Giles."

Jeff couldn't believe his ears. He started dancing around with She'a. Mindy and K.J. joined in too. Even Warren and Dr. Jones got in the act.

A moment later, Dr. Jones tried to stand still to explain everything to Chief Naati and the people. Then everyone started dancing and singing.

Jeff stopped. He looked over at his new friend She'a, then up to heaven. Tears filled his eyes as he whispered an apology to God for his unbelief.

He was totally amazed.

God had come through again.

Other
Reel Kids Adventures
by Dave Gustaveson

The Missing Video
An exciting adventure into Communist Cuba. Will the dark-eyes stranger send the *Reel Kids* into an international nightmare?

Mystery at Smokey Mountain
A spine-tingling mystery with the *Reel Kids* in the Philippines. Jeff and the "Reel Kids" become the target of wicked men as they attempt to help the poor at Smokey Mountain in Manila.

The Stolen Necklace
A stolen necklace, wild animals and a life threatening African mystery will keep *Reel Kids* readers turning pages.

The Mysterious Case
Jeff Caldwell couldn't imagine how one small mistake would cost them. A mysterious suitcase leads them on a collision course with the dangerous Colombian drug cartel. Would the drug lords allow them to continue their mission?

COMING SOON!
Another *Reel Kids* adventure on the seas, *The Dangerous Voyage.*

OTHER RESOURCES:

You Can Change the World — $14.99
Colorful illustrations, facts, and stories help you understand and pray for people in other coultures and countries.

Tracking Your Walk — $9.99
This journal will help you record your prayers and thoughts and encourages you to pray for people around the world. Includes maps and country information.

For more information on missions work in the Amazon, write to:
Tribal Ministries
Caixa Postal 441
Port Velho, Rondonia 78.900.970
Brazil

For information to help you go on your own adventure:
Kings Kids
P.O. Box 8000-569
Sumas, WA 98295

For Youth With A Mission's outreach opportunities, send for the *GO MANUAL*.
Send $4.00 to:
YWAM Publishing
P.O. Box 55787
Seattle, WA 98155